'I shouldn't want you—I can't want you—but I do.'

Zafir kissed her neck and she leant her head back against him, allowing him more access. A shiver of anticipation darted around her body as his lips touched every bit of naked skin on her neck.

'Neither of us should want this, but we do.' Destiny's words were a ragged whisper as her heart thudded in her chest. She wanted to turn to him, to press her lips against his, but at the same time couldn't break the tenuous contact they now shared. 'Let's just forget the rest of the world for a few hours—forget everything except what we feel now.'

His kisses stilled and she felt his chest expanding against her back with every deep breath he took. Had she said too much—again?

'I want to forget it all,' he said, and pressed his lips into her hair, inhaling deeply as if taking in her scent. 'I want you in a way I've never wanted a woman before. But I can't be like other men. I have a duty to my country.'

'Just for these hours of darkness,' she whispered, and opened her eyes to look once again at the stars. 'That's all we need, Zafir, just one night.'

Rachael Thomas has always loved reading romance, and is thrilled to be a Mills & Boon author. She lives and works on a farm in Wales—a far cry from the glamour of a Mills & Boon Modern story—but that makes slipping into her characters' worlds all the more appealing. When she's not writing, or working on the farm, she enjoys photography and visiting historical castles and grand houses. Visit her at rachaelthomas.co.uk.

Books by Rachael Thomas

Mills & Boon Modern Romance

New Year at the Boss's Bidding
From One Night to Wife
Craving Her Enemy's Touch
Claimed by the Sheikh
A Deal Before the Altar

Visit the Author Profile page at
millsandboon.co.uk for more titles.

THE SHEIKH'S
LAST MISTRESS

BY
RACHAEL THOMAS

First Published in Great Britain 2016
By Mills & Boon, an imprint of HarperCollins*Publishers*
1 London Bridge Street, London, SE1 9GF

© 2016 Rachael Thomas

ISBN: 978-0-263-26417-3

Our policy is to use papers that are natural, renewable and recyclable
products and made from wood grown in sustainable forests. The logging
and manufacturing processes conform to the legal environmental
regulations of the country of origin.

Printed and bound in Great Britain
by CPI Antony Rowe, Chippenham, Wiltshire

20379074

THE SHEIKH'S
LAST MISTRESS

For James, Marian and David.

CHAPTER ONE

Zafir Al Asmari was sceptical as he drove towards the old red-brick house, which was a stark contrast to the immaculate penthouse he'd just left in London. Was it possible the woman he was seeking really worked here? This riding school, nestled in the countryside beyond London, certainly looked as if it had seen better days— not at all where he had imagined finding Destiny Richards. Her reputation with difficult horses had made him travel from Kezoban personally to seek her out.

He parked his black sports car and got out, unsure if he should even continue with this madness. He must have been misinformed. Destiny Richards wouldn't be working somewhere so ordinary. Nothing about the old house or tired-looking sheds gave any hint of being professional stables. He was on the point of leaving when movement inside the shed beyond the house caught his eye.

Zafir walked forward, his shoes crunching on the grit of the driveway, and, unable to contain his curiosity, looked into the building being used as the riding school. Through an open door, he could see a tall, slim young woman lunging a chestnut horse around her. Intrigued, he walked down the side of the house, intent on seeing exactly who this woman was. If she was Destiny Richards, he could settle his unease and confirm he'd done the right thing by hiring her before coming to meet her personally.

'Ah, you have arrived.' A sharp female voice behind him dragged his attention from the young woman and horse. He stopped, turning abruptly to an older and somewhat overenthusiastic woman. 'Are you here for the Sheikh? To see Destiny work her magic?'

Zafir narrowed his eyes. Instinct warned him of this woman's insincerity. Her overzealous attitude jarred his nerves, but if she thought he was here for the Sheikh instead of actually being the Sheikh, then so much the better. He could ascertain if Destiny Richards did indeed possess the gift of horse whispering, something he very much hoped was true, but right now, given the surroundings, he was inclined to think he'd been misled.

'I am and I don't have time to waste. Where is Ms Richards?'

'My daughter is in the school. This way.' She gestured with a smile which didn't reach her eyes, backing up his first impression. It didn't bode well that Destiny Richards was this woman's daughter. First impressions counted for a lot in his culture and he was far from impressed, but had to remember this might be Majeed's last chance.

Without another word, he made his way to the school, aware the woman was following. Quietly he entered, stood against the wooden interior wall and watched. For a while the young woman he now knew was Destiny Richards had no idea he was there and he couldn't help his gaze sweeping over her, appreciating her tall and shapely figure and how the tight-fitting jodhpurs and T-shirt clung, in a way only a hot-blooded male could, just as he'd always done before duty had brought him to heel.

Her dark hair was pulled up high on her head into a ponytail, which swayed like a dancer to an unheard tune with each move she made. She was distracting and not at all what he'd expected, especially after having just met her mother.

The horse slowed to a walk, then stopped at her calm command. Destiny waited for the horse to walk to her and, as she touched its face, Zafir could hear the sound of soothing words, seeing the obvious connection of trust the horse had with her. Then she turned round, her eyes meeting his instantly.

Despite the distance something passed between them, jolting him with its intensity. She was beautiful and, for the first time since he'd inherited the title of Sheikh of Kezoban, he felt his interest stirring, awakening everything he'd turned his back on. He pushed that thought aside. Now was not the time to be distracted by a woman, not when Royal protocol dictated he had to select a bride. As the last remaining member of his family, providing his country with an heir was paramount.

'Destiny, this man is here for the Sheikh. You know, the one we told you about.' The older woman's voice held a hint of warning, despite her smile, and the sudden tension in the air between mother and daughter was palpable, like storm clouds about to break over a hot city.

He crossed the sandy surface towards Destiny as her mother continued to talk. He was sure he saw a flash of defiance rush across Destiny's beautiful face as she glanced briefly at her mother before looking at him once more. Her fine brows arched in disbelief and her lips set into a firm line of disapproval. He couldn't help wondering what kissing away that disapproval would be like, confident it would be as intense as the attraction he felt for her.

'I remember.' Her voice was soft and gentle, but he didn't miss the underlying note of determination. She stepped towards him, the horse moving with her, staying loyally at her side as she offered her hand in a Western handshake and smiled at him. 'Destiny Richards. How can I help you?'

A smile pulled at the corners of his lips. He liked the feisty spirit she was working hard to conceal, reminding him of a young horse that would rather run free with the wind across the desert sands than be confined and controlled. He'd had to put such ideas to one side after his father had died six years ago, his days of being the wild playboy Sheikh his father despaired of abruptly curtailed. For the first time since that day he wished he was free; the attraction for this woman was so intense all he could do was imagine taking her in his arms and kissing away her defiance.

He took her hand and the jolt of something new and exciting sizzled through him. The deep brown of her eyes, which reminded him of polished mahogany, mirrored the attraction. 'Forgive me for the intrusion. Your ability to work with horses that have been traumatised has come to the attention of the Sheikh of Kezoban. He has made an arrangement with the owners here for you to travel to Kezoban to work with his prized Arabian stallion, but he sent me to personally meet you before my return.'

The deceit slipped easily from him. He was preserving his sanity by omitting the truth, sure that her mother would make matters far worse for him and probably Destiny if she knew his true identity.

'I see. And if I don't wish to travel to Kezoban?' That firm edge in her voice was more pronounced now.

'Then we will have a problem. It is all arranged— subject to my confirmation that you are as gifted with horses as the Sheikh has been led to believe.' Zafir pressed his lips firmly together as Destiny's spirit shone through. Would she have spoken to him in such an honest and open way if she'd known he was the Sheikh, the man who'd made the deal for her presence in Kezoban?

'I have to see the horse first before I commit or agree to anything.' Was that a challenge he saw glittering in those dark eyes? He liked a challenge. He raised his brows in a silent answer.

'Destiny! What are you doing?' Her mother's shock was obvious. So too was his. He'd almost forgotten she was there. For a few brief moments as he and Destiny had spoken, it had just been the two of them. Nothing else had existed. The exclusive contact between him and a woman was not a sensation he was accustomed to at all.

'You may leave us.' The command in his voice was brittle as he turned his attention to the older woman, but it worked. She bowed her head very slightly in deference to him and backed away. So Destiny hadn't inherited her spirit from her mother.

'If you will excuse me, I need to deal with this horse.' Destiny didn't wait for his consent, but walked away. He stood and watched her go, slightly unnerved by the fight for control he was experiencing, a totally new concept for him.

Determined to settle the agreement, Zafir followed at a distance as Destiny led the chestnut horse out of the school. Usually he was more than able to appreciate good horse stock, but right now his attention was riveted to the very alluring woman leading the horse. Her strong will and defiance stirred something deep inside him, something he had shut out of his life years ago.

Desire.

Why this woman? She was beautiful, but not in the glamorous way he'd liked his women before his days as Kezoban's ruler. She had an earthy innocence about her and was far from compliant if the last minutes were anything to go by, but there was something which had connected to a forgotten and neglected part of him the second their eyes had met.

She walked the horse into a stable, shutting the door, making it clear he was to stay outside. He leant his arms on the top of the stable door, watching as she untacked the horse and brushed it down, her gently rhythmic movements appreciated by the animal as it pulled hay from the rack, munching noisily.

'So, have I passed the test?' She paused and looked at him over the back of the horse, directly into his eyes. Again he had the distinct impression a challenge was being laid down—and he never refused a challenge.

'Yes. I have seen enough.'

'But you have not passed my test.' She angled her head slightly, her ponytail swinging gently. 'I want to know exactly what is expected of me.'

Zafir could only admire her courage. Nobody challenged him. Ever. Would she have been so unguarded if she knew who he was? Briefly he was tempted to tell her, but he was enjoying this sparring so he decided to allow her to continue under the misapprehension of his identity that her mother had started. He had no wish to set her right just yet.

'You will travel to Kezoban where you will work with Majeed, the Sheikh's prized stallion.'

She looked at him, her brown eyes regarding him warily as she resumed brushing the horse. Zafir didn't appreciate the look of mistrust in those deliciously dark eyes, but he had no option other than to wait patiently for her response—and waiting was something he was not used to.

'What is the problem with the stallion?' She glanced briefly at him as she finished with the horse and came to the stable door.

Zafir stood back to allow her out, shocked that already her question was dragging up the past. He knew that would have to happen if he ever stood a chance of soothing Majeed's tortured spirit, but he hadn't expected it to be so soon. Neither had he envisaged being under her scrutiny.

'The stallion was involved in a tragic accident which claimed the life of the Sheikh's sister.' He was strangely detached as he spoke of his sister, referring to that night as if it hadn't really happened. Despite this temporary reprieve from guilt, he knew it didn't lessen the blame he'd set firmly at his own feet. He was the one Tabinah had been running from, the one who had made her unhappy. The knowledge of that would never leave him.

Destiny looked at the handsome man who seemed somehow unsuited to the jeans which hugged his long legs and the light blue shirt, open at the neck, giving her a tantalising view of dark hair against olive skin. She already knew him to be a man of the desert and, despite his casual clothes, she could just imagine him in white robes. He had a raw essence of power about him and was handsome enough to melt her vulnerable heart. But from the upright stance of his body and the regal tilt of his chin, she knew he was also very much used to giving orders—and having them obeyed.

Well, she wasn't about to be ordered around by anyone. She'd had enough of being the one who always had to give in to the demands of others. Her stepmother had gone too far this time, accepting the job before she'd even spoken to her. Everything was about money for her, never the person and least of all the horse involved.

Her stepmother was as cold as her father and equally controlling, which only reinforced Destiny's need to escape them. She couldn't stay here any longer. The stables might be entwined with precious childhood memories of her mother and the few short years of happiness before her death, but she had to leave. Just as her younger sister, Milly, had done. And she had to do it before her stepmother completely obliterated those happy memories.

'I'm very sorry about the situation the Sheikh is in, but I cannot help.' She kept her gaze locked with his, trying to meet his aura of power with determination, wanting to convey the message that she would not be controlled—not any more.

His eyes, as black as onyx, narrowed with irritation and his jaw clenched beneath the dark trimmed beard, so precise it was barely more than stubble. 'That is not the arrangement I have come to with Mrs Richards. She

assured me you would be available to travel to Kezoban immediately.'

The words fired out at her but she stood her ground,
adamant she would not to be ordered around be either
this superior man or her stepmother.

'Firstly, I am her stepdaughter and, secondly, she
had no right to make any such arrangement without
consulting me. Not even with a wealthy Sheikh. So I
suggest you look elsewhere for the help you require.'

She moved towards him, intending to walk past him
and away, wanting only to turn her back on this man
who exuded a potent mix of masculinity and sexual-
ity which terrified yet enthralled her. His eyes, full of
fiery intensity, met hers as she came level with him,
but it was the enticing aura of this powerful man as
she came close—too close—that made her step falter.
It became impossible to do anything other than stand
and look directly into his handsome face.

Her stomach somersaulted and, like a teenager in
the throes of a first love, her heart skipped a beat. Not
that she knew anything about first love, having shied
away from all that, using horses as her shield. She was
angry with her stepmother and not at all affected by
this exotic man. She reminded herself of that fact, but
struggled as his gaze continued to hold hers.

'The deal is agreed, Miss Richards. You will travel
to Kezoban in two days.' The control in his voice, the
hardened words and the command he exuded made
anything other than looking up at him impossible, even
though she wanted to get as far away from the effect
he was having on her as possible. The anger glittering
in the blackness of his eyes reminded her of the night
sky, full of stars.

For the last sixteen years, since her stepmother had become a permanent feature in her and her younger sister's lives, she'd done her stepmother's and father's bidding, putting aside all of her dreams and aspirations. She'd wanted to be there for Milly as she grew up but more recently it had become all about helping Milly set herself up in London and escape their father's oppressive control. Now that Milly was settled and happy it was time she did the same.

Milly had left home earlier in the year and there was no one to protect now, no one to look out for but herself. She was free to do what she wanted. Now this man, with his high-handed attitude, thought he could waltz in and more or less demand she go to a desert country because it was what his Sheikh wanted. Surely the Sheikh had enough money to hire the top professionals in the field.

Could this man, this bizarre offer to travel to a desert kingdom she knew nothing about, be her opportunity of escape?

Her love of horses had been all-consuming as she'd grown up, leaving no room for any other kind of love and giving her the perfect excuse to escape from reality. Could she use her ability to connect with horses as her means of escape?

'I don't care what deal you have made. I will not go.' The words flew from her lips as the oppression of living under her father's strict rule surfaced. Going to an unknown country at the request of another equally controlling man was not something she'd planned for herself. All she wanted was to get away and as tempting as this offer was, it wasn't what she needed. She would find another way to gain her financial independence and ultimately her freedom.

'Majeed is a majestic creature. He wants only to please.' His words cut through her thoughts, tugging at those emotional heartstrings she always had for an animal. 'It is as if he knows the woman who rode him into the desert and fell from his back was the Sheikh's sister, as if he blames himself.'

Destiny looked up at him, her interest captured as she imagined the horse, but she couldn't be drawn into this man's problems. She had her own to solve.

'She died.' The words were hard and short, the pain within them tugging at her sentimental heart. He must genuinely love the horse and want to serve his master.

'I'm sorry for the Sheikh's loss, but really I cannot help.' Still she clung firmly to her refusal.

'The horse is living in torment. He is unapproachable, almost impossible to handle and a danger to himself and others. It has been a year since the accident. Many have tried to calm his troubled spirit. You are the Sheikh's last hope and if you cannot help Majeed there is only one other option.'

She drew in a sharp breath as the implications of his words hit her. He could stand there all day and argue about the deal he'd made with her stepmother and she wouldn't care, wouldn't back down. But as soon as he'd talked of the stallion, the compassion in his voice showing he at least cared about the horse and its fate, she knew she would go. But she wasn't about to let this man know that yet, not when she had her own deal to strike, one that would finally set her free from a life she would never have chosen for herself.

'What are the terms of the agreement you have

made?' She continued to stand glaring up him, the injustice of her situation filling her with the kind of courage which had evaded her for many years.

'The arrangement is that you will travel to Kezoban for a minimum of two months, to work with the stallion. A substantial amount of money has already been agreed.' His tone remained as commanding as ever, but something in his expression softened slightly. Was it possible a hard man such as this could soften? No, she must be mistaken. He was as dominating and controlling as her father. She might be about to use him as a chance to escape her father's iron rule, but she was under no illusions: this man was the epitome of supremacy. Her terms needed to be laid firmly down.

'This substantial amount of money has been agreed with my stepmother, no doubt.' Destiny tried to keep the icy coldness from her voice as she thought of the woman who had replaced her mother. She knew now that her father had never been happy and loving, as she'd thought when she was a young child. That had all been pretence. The day her mother had died, everything changed. He'd stopped pretending. He'd become cold and mercenary, finally meeting his match in his new wife. Now he was allowing her stepmother to use his daughter's gift to extract money from the Sheikh of a far-off desert kingdom.

'It has, yes. To cover your absence here. You are a valued member of her team.' The man's words remained gentle and coaxing, maybe because he sensed her impending agreement. But his chosen words made her want to laugh out loud. Her stepmother did not value her, always reminding her she was nothing, just a stable girl. It was the money such a deal would generate she valued.

But Destiny couldn't let him know that his Sheikh's offer was going to be her way out, her chance to finally to do what she wanted in life and travel. If she could help the Sheikh's stallion in the process, all the better. It was, after all, something she was good at.

'I will, of course, have expenses to cover.' She knew she would never see any form of payment from her stepmother or the business; creating her own expenses was the only way to enable her to return to England and start a new life with money of her own. 'Double the original payment should be sufficient—and paid to me.'

'Naturally.' Was that a hint of sarcasm in his deep voice? His dark eyes narrowed slightly in suspicion and she thought she'd gone too far.

'I would need to see the horse first.' She kept her tone brisk, her gaze fixed on his handsome face, hardly able to believe he was accepting the conditions she was attaching to the agreement.

'In that case, my private jet will be at your disposal to fly you to Kezoban as soon as you are ready.' A smile of satisfaction touched his lips and those intensely dark eyes held hers, sending that spark rushing through her again, but she pushed the sensation aside, wanting only to ignore it.

'Your private jet?' Surely an aide to a Sheikh wouldn't have his own private jet? He must have meant the Sheikh's jet, but such details were insignificant now. Her much longed for escape from the ties of her father's rule were on the horizon and excitement fizzed inside her so much that she couldn't help but smile up at this strikingly handsome stranger who'd somehow turned her world upside down.

Zafir was on the verge of confessing that he was the Sheikh, that he'd allowed her to continue with her assumption that he was merely an aide sent to ascertain her ability, but, despite the brightness of her smile, the suspicion in her voice as she'd questioned his last words held him back. He couldn't risk her turning down his offer, not when his most precious horse still lived the nightmare of the night his sister had died. Everything in his life had spiralled out of control after that night and it was beyond time to put it right.

The marriage he'd known for years he'd have to make was looming, but Tabinah's death last year had put even more pressure on him to do his duty. And he would, once Majeed was healed. Only then could he put the nightmare of his sister's unhappiness at the marriage he'd arranged for her aside and fulfil his duty to make his own arranged marriage.

'My apology—the Sheikh's private jet.' His words were sharp but, lost in her own thoughts, she didn't notice. 'Do we have a deal, Miss Richards?'

He pushed down the guilt and shame of the night his sister had fled the palace. He would do anything to turn back the clock to the day he'd all but ordered Tabinah to do her duty and marry the man he'd selected for her. He hadn't been a brother to his younger sister, hadn't known how desperately unhappy she was. He'd just been the ruler of Kezoban, unaware she'd hated him, wanting only to shut him out of her life. The guilt that he'd made her so unhappy would always remain with him, even as he tried to piece his life together again, but soothing the tortured spirit of his stallion Majeed would help him finally put that night in the past.

He looked at Destiny, her soft brown eyes full of compassion, despite her bravado in standing up to him. Not only was he sure she possessed the gift to heal Majeed, he was certain she had the kindness in her heart the horse needed, unlike the others who had tried and failed.

'Yes, we do. I can be ready to leave in two days.'

Zafir offered his hand, wanting to seal the deal and return to his homeland. The dark-haired woman who'd captured his attention in more ways than one took his hand and the warmth from hers spread through him. It was as if their spirits were joining, recognising one another on an as yet undiscovered level. She looked up at him and the same confusion which consumed him blazed in her eyes.

Did she feel the pull of attraction too? Did she feel the connection, as if they knew one another, knew that they were fated to cross paths?

He pushed the thought aside. He didn't have the luxury of choosing his path through life, and this woman, whilst the kind of distraction he would have sought once, was not what he needed now—or ever again.

She intrigued him in a way no woman had ever done and, after the tragedy of the last twelve months, he liked the way she made him feel as her eyes met his. She was as spirited as a stallion and yet as nervous as a young filly foal. Today she'd been bold and fearless addressing him, but what would she be like once in Kezoban? Would she still have that feisty spark when she knew *he* was the Sheikh?

'Very well. I will return and prepare for your arrival.'

'And if I feel that I am unable to help the stallion?' Her hesitation lingered in the air. 'Can I leave?'

'You will not be a prisoner, Miss Richards. You will be the Sheikh's honoured guest and may leave whenever you wish.'

CHAPTER TWO

DESTINY LOOKED DOWN at the arid landscape below as the jet prepared for landing. The old town, seemingly carved from the desert, rose up around a rocky hill and next to a river; on the other side was a building of such splendour it could only be the Sheikh of Kezoban's palace. Around it, newer and more prosperous-looking buildings nestled, as if for safety, and beyond that lay an expanse of desert. Everything intrigued her and she wished she'd had more time for researching the place before she'd left England.

As the sumptuous jet touched down her excitement grew. This was to be her home for the next two months and, if she was really honest with herself, she was somewhat naively looking forward to seeing the Sheikh's aide again. It was only after he'd left the stables she'd realised she had been so intent on taking charge of her life she had no idea of his name. It had been his job, she'd reassured herself, to be controlling and demanding. Then there had been the moment he'd taken her hand, the memory of it still tugging at her unfulfilled romantic dreams.

There had been something about him, other than his undeniable good looks, and she'd been drawn to him with an attraction she'd never indulged in before. Despite the control he exuded, she'd briefly seen a different man as he'd spoken of the Sheikh's stallion. Then the hard exterior had slipped back into place, shielding the real man from her scrutiny.

This thought still played out in her mind as she left the cool air-conditioned interior of the jet and stepped out into the desert of Kezoban. Instantly a wall of heat almost pressed her back into the jet but, as a black SUV pulled up alongside the steps of the jet, she descended, hoping to see at least one familiar face.

She was alarmed, not just at her disappointment but that the man who'd come to the stables wasn't there. To hide it, she pulled the fine cream scarf she'd chosen to use as a headscarf a little tighter against her face and got into the SUV as the door was opened for her by a man in desert robes who seemed completely indifferent to her. If this was her welcome, what would the Sheikh be like when they finally met?

The drive from the airfield was short and she tried to glimpse the scenery as they passed from the dry desert land to the town. The streets were busy with people going about their daily lives and she longed to be among them—the anonymity, exploring the vibrant market. Soon the imposing walls of the palace loomed ahead of them and her stomach flipped over with nerves.

She was ushered from the SUV up cool marble steps and into the palace, where she was swept along by an entourage that made taking in anything more than a glimpse of the intricate and ornate design of the palace impossible. Her anxiety level rose as two large doors were swept open before them and all but two members of her escort left.

She just had time to glance around the high-ceilinged room, admire the blue and gold designs and the view into what must be the palace gardens before another set of doors opposite her opened.

The relief she felt at seeing the Sheikh's aide almost made her sigh, but that relief quickly changed to confusion as those around him bowed their heads and stepped back, leaving them alone but for the two men standing like guards by the door she'd entered.

She looked at the handsome face, framed by the white headdress he wore which served only to heighten his handsome features. His midnight black eyes looked directly into hers and she couldn't say anything as he walked towards her. His robes suited him far more than the jeans and shirt she'd first seen him in. With fine gold cloth over the robes, he looked positively regal.

'Allow me to introduce myself.' He spoke with a calm accented voice that had the velvety edge to it she remembered from that afternoon at the stables. 'I am Sheikh Zafir Al Asmari of Kezoban.'

Destiny fought against confusion, her words almost faltering. 'The Sheikh's aide?'

'No. The Sheikh.'

He had never told her his name, but he had definitely allowed her to believe he was the Sheikh's aide. Had he been testing her?

'It would have been nice to have known exactly who I was speaking to when you visited the stables.'

She should probably have spoken with more respect and, judging by his expression, he had expected her to. He took another step towards her and she tried to quell the tremor of attraction she felt for him, just as she had done that day at the stables. Even when she'd believed he was just the Sheikh's aide she'd known he would never notice someone like her, but that hadn't stopped the romantic in her dreaming of being swept away to his kingdom instead of being ordered there. Now she knew exactly who he was those romantic notions were about as likely as getting drenched from a storm cloud bursting above her head right now.

Everything about him suggested power and control; she just hadn't wanted to admit it—not when it put him in the same league as her father. Now it was worse. He wasn't just an aide to the Sheikh; he *was* the Sheikh. A leader. A man who should have power, and she despised controlling men. So why did her stomach flutter as his dark eyes locked with hers before his gaze slid down her body? She stood tall beneath his scrutiny, glad she'd opted to dress in keeping with the country's culture.

'It was your assumption that I visited on behalf of the Sheikh of Kezoban. I did not intend to mislead you and for that I apologise. Your stepmother made the assumption and I allowed it to continue.' He moved closer but she remained where she was, determined not to be intimidated by him. 'I trust we can move forward from the misunderstanding.'

His accented words were faultless English, his ability to use the language impressive, but it only added to his aura of command, the same command that had been absent as he'd talked of the Sheikh's sister—his sister. She'd assumed he'd been thinking about the stallion as emotion and pain had filled his words in England. He'd seen through her stepmother, making him seem more human, more feeling, and that was something this man, who stood regally watching her, could never be.

'I am here to work with your stallion, not pass judgement on you.' She lifted her chin and tried to ignore the sizzle racing around her body as his gaze locked with hers once more.

As she'd accepted the contract to work for this man she'd thought it was like stepping out of the shadow of her father's iron will and into the furnace of a much greater force. How right that had been. His ability to allow her to believe he was merely an aide to the Sheikh reinforced that, but working for the Sheikh was a gateway through which she must travel in order to start her new and independent life. It was the chance she'd been seeking and one she would take, no matter what.

When Destiny had been shown into his office Zafir had been overwhelmed to see her dressed modestly with respect for his culture. It should have stopped the hot thud of attraction which had surged through him from the moment he'd first seen her in England, but it didn't; it only served to intensify it. That day at the stables something had ignited between them and, if he wasn't mistaken, she was as reluctant to admit its presence as he was. Which only fuelled his ardour and intensified his curiosity to sample the forbidden.

'You have had a long journey. Tomorrow you will meet Majeed and begin your work. Tonight, as my guest, you will dine with me.' It was customary for him to dine with visitors but, from the look on her face, it was the last thing she'd expected.

She regarded him suspiciously and he fought the

need to smile. This was the first time he'd encountered a woman's reluctance to dine with him, but then he'd never invited a woman from another culture into his palace. Prior to inheriting the title of Sheikh of Kezoban he'd always kept his affairs confined to either London or New York.

'Thank you, but I am sure you have far more important things to do than entertain me.' Again the spark of fire leapt to life within him as her soft voice all but caressed his senses. He must have been living with the weight of duty for too long because he'd almost forgotten what such a sizzle of attraction could do to him. But never had it been so insistent.

'I always entertain my guests, Miss Richards. You will not be an exception.'

'Is it absolutely necessary?' The question was accompanied by the lift of her delicate eyebrows, but the courage of it didn't go unnoticed. Nobody would dare to address him like that, question his orders. He should be angry, should be making her error known, but he didn't want to. She wasn't speaking to him as Zafir the Sheikh but Zafir the man. Since he'd taken on the role of Sheikh of Kezoban after his father's death, no man or woman had treated him as anything other than that.

'It is.' He moved a little closer to her so that he could inhale her light floral scent and wished he'd dismissed everyone from the room. Right now all he wanted was to kiss her, taste the sweetness of those full lips.

He stepped back. What was he thinking? He was a desert ruler, a man of power with a duty to uphold. Kissing this woman, however much he wanted to, was not something he could ever do, especially when she was here in his palace as his guest.

'Then I look forward to it.'

'As will I.' It was the truth; he wanted to spend the evening in her company. 'We have much to discuss about your intended work with Majeed.'

He walked back to his large and ornate desk, where he turned and faced her once more. Distance was most definitely needed between him and this beautiful Western woman who had stirred the emotions and wild desires of the man he used to be.

'I appreciate it will be painful for you, but I will need to know all about what happened that night and how the stallion was before the accident.'

'And you shall.' But only what he absolutely had to say. He could never confess to anyone that he'd been guilty of neglecting his young sister so terribly. That the marriage he'd insisted she make had forced her to take such drastic steps. No, he could never allow anyone to know that. For the last year he'd been in the grip of that guilt and the way this woman was making him feel intensified it. He had no right to desire any woman when he was about to make an arranged marriage, not after insisting Tabinah did the same.

Destiny's nerves fluttered as she followed her escort through the cool interior of the palace to join the man she now had to keep reminding herself was the Sheikh of Kezoban. A man who had concealed his true identity, but she couldn't yet understand what he had to gain from that—apart from control.

She should have been able to relax in the luxury of her suite, with its views over the stunning palace gardens, but the thought of spending the evening with a man who intrigued and excited her as much as he irritated her with his need for control meant she was far from relaxed.

Darkness was falling and the palace was lit with lanterns at each of the ornate archways she passed through, giving everything a dreamlike quality. Then her escort stepped aside and gestured her through an arched doorway and along a vast walkway to another part of the palace gardens. She could see what resembled tents, draped almost completely in pale gold chiffon; lanterns glowed inside. It looked far too intimate for a formal dinner with the man who was effectively her boss for the next two months.

Then she saw him, his headdress discarded, giving him a more relaxed look, and her pulse leapt. Since when did the sight of a man do that to her?

'Good evening. I trust you are rested from your journey.' His deep sensual voice matched the mood created by his chosen venue for their meal and a brief skitter of panic raced over her before she dismissed it. As if this powerful Sheikh would be remotely interested in her. He probably had a harem of beautiful women.

'With such a gorgeous suite, how could I not be?' She couldn't look directly at him as heat infused her cheeks.

When she did glance his way, it was to see his lips lifting upwards in a smile, one that sent a spark of amusement to his dark eyes. It was the first time she'd seen anything other than a severe or commanding expression on his face. It was also a smile that would melt hearts, hers included if the heady beat of her pulse was anything to go by.

'I appreciate the effort you made today.' She frowned at him, not sure what he was referring to. 'You dressed to fit in with my culture and so this evening I wanted to show you a sample of life in the desert.'

'Thank you.' She forced the words out, totally taken aback by his thoughtfulness. Not at all what she would have expected from the man who had all but demanded she come to his country or the man who'd stood in his office just hours ago, an aura of power surrounding him.

'I only regret I could not have shown you the real desert.'

'This is lovely,' she said as she walked into the tent. The warm night air played with the pale gold curtains and candles glowed within ornate lanterns, lending a romantic ambience to the setting.

Should she be worried by this gesture? She glanced anxiously at the man she knew very little about—she had placed herself at his mercy, thousands of miles from home. Who was she trying to fool? This was a desert king. A man whose life was so different from hers he would never think inappropriately of someone like her and the sooner she got that idea fixed in her head the better.

'Does it not please you?' A hint of a feral growl sounded in his voice and she realised her silence had cast doubt on her appreciation of all he'd done.

'It's perfect. Utterly beautiful.'

Zafir watched as Destiny, wearing loose-fitting white trousers and a long top, looked around. The pale pink scarf she wore on her head made her appear as delicate as a bloom in his prized gardens. She took in every detail and he found himself wishing they were in the middle of the desert, far away from anyone and, even more importantly, his duty. Not that family duty and honour were a trait she understood if the tension between her and her stepmother were anything to go by. She was here under duress and she'd clearly stated her terms, but that didn't stop the sizzle of desire which flowed through him like the river his city was built around.

He wanted to tell her she was more beautiful than anything around them, but he hadn't brought her here to seduce her. This was his palace, his home and he'd never entertained any woman here, even throughout his wild playboy days. He also needed to remind himself of the marriage he had to make. This was a woman he couldn't afford to be distracted by for so many reasons.

'I'm pleased you approve.' He kept his voice as neutral as possible in an attempt to hide the effect she was having on him.

'I'm also looking forward to seeing your stallion tomorrow.' She glanced at him and he saw the apprehension on her face before she spoke again. 'I do need to know more of the incident.'

'By "incident" you mean the night my sister rode him out into the desert and met with her untimely death?' This was the last thing he wanted to talk about. All the guilt from that night rushed back at him. He would have to share a certain amount of information with Destiny, but he wasn't ready yet to reveal everything.

'If I am to help the horse then I am afraid I need to know.'

The sympathy on her face only made his guilt worse. She must think he was so heartbroken after the loss of his sister that he couldn't talk about it. Nothing could be further from the truth and nothing would make him admit the guilt he harboured.

'First we eat,' he said as his servants arrived with their meal. He gestured to the table, set with his colours, the same bright purple and gold that would adorn his private tent when he spent time in the desert, something he did several times a year.

She smiled at him and he could see his brusque tone had unsettled her, but it was necessary. Duty meant he could never let his emotions influence any decision he made. Duty also meant he could never have needs himself. It was always at the forefront of everything he did, just as it had been when he'd arranged Tabinah's marriage, resisting her pleas for him to reconsider.

'This is not what I expected to be doing this evening,' she said as she settled herself on the cushions around the low table. The excitement on her face made her skin glow and her eyes sparkle. She was even more beautiful than he remembered. Just as when he'd first met her, she appeared totally unaware of her beauty, almost as if she was intent on hiding or remaining out of the spotlight.

'What did you expect? That I would banish you to your room and lock you up unless you were working with Majeed?' Although it was meant in jest, he was shocked to see her cheeks flush with colour.

'No, not that,' she said softly, a hint of nerves in her voice. 'I just didn't expect such special treatment or the effort you've gone to.'

'You are here as my guest, Destiny.' It was the first time he'd used her name in conversation and it all but sizzled on his tongue and a spark of lust hurtled through him. 'I like to show all my guests what my kingdom and its people can offer.'

He had to add that, had to try and refocus his attention away from the way she was making him feel as she sat opposite him, her partially visible dark hair gleaming in the light from the lanterns and looking so soft he wanted to touch it, to feel its silkiness and slide it through his fingers as his lips claimed hers.

What was he thinking? He should not be entertaining such thoughts. Not just because she was here to do a job, or even because she was a woman from a different culture. He could never think about any woman that way, not even the woman he was soon to select as his bride.

'I am here to do a job.' Her words were stronger, confidence filling them as they had done the first time he'd met her. 'And to do that I need to know about certain events.'

He waited whilst his servants cleared the table and watched her face fill with delight and disbelief as an array of desserts were placed between them. As the servants quietly withdrew he wished Destiny was here as his guest, wished that he didn't have to reveal anything about the night Tabinah died. Inexplicably, it mattered what this woman thought of him.

'Tabinah was unhappy with the man I had chosen for her to marry. It was a marriage of duty on both sides, uniting two wealthy and powerful families. Unfortunately, Tabinah didn't share my view on duty. She wanted nothing but her freedom.'

'Her freedom?' Destiny's brows drew together as she tried to process the information, confusion clear on her face.

'She claimed to be in love with another man, one totally unsuitable for the sister of the Sheikh of Kezoban.' His words were dry and monotone. It was the first time he'd told anyone that his young sister had declared her love for a man other than the one she was engaged to. He knew it was talked of within the palace. He was no fool. He'd heard the whispered speculations. He'd just never admitted it to anyone before.

'I'm sorry.' She lowered her lashes, obviously embarrassed to look at him.

'It is of no consequence. Many arranged marriages do not contain any love at all,' he stated flatly as he wiped his fingers and signalled for the remains of their meal to be cleared.

'It is sad.' She looked directly at him and he had the distinct impression she was challenging him. How, he wasn't yet sure. 'Everybody needs love.'

'Have you ever been in love, Destiny?' He narrowed his eyes as anger simmered beneath his cool composure. So she believed in love and probably believed in fairy tales where everyone lived happily ever after. He, however, believed in real life.

'I have love in my life, yes.' The defensive tone of her voice goaded him to prod for more.

'As do I. Love for my people, my country and my family honour, but that is not what I asked. Have you ever believed you were in love?' Suddenly it mattered that she had the same foolish notions as Tabinah, that she was filling her head with romantic dreams of happiness.

'No.' Destiny fired the answer back at him, not liking the way his dark eyes were watching every move she made, every expression which crossed her face. She'd seen love in her mother's diary, felt it as she read the pages, but the fact that her father had remarried so soon after her mother had died told her all she needed to know. Her mother had loved, but had never been loved. Something she would never allow to happen to her. She would only give her heart to a man who loved her completely.

'And you have not married,' he said. It wasn't a question and silently she watched him. His expression was stern.

'My work has kept me busy.'

She followed his lead and stood up from the table, but when he approached her she couldn't ignore the sudden racing of her heart. She wanted to back away, give herself space, but his dark gaze held hers, mesmerising her.

'You shouldn't hide behind your work.' His voice was deep and sensuous and that little tremor she'd felt when she'd first seen him slipped down her spine again.

'I don't.' She couldn't help how defensive her voice sounded. 'I love my work. It's more than just work and that's why I'm here. I came here for your horse, not because my stepmother arranged it or because you demanded it, but to help your horse.'

For a moment she thought she'd gone too far, crossed that invisible line of protocol which she had realised surrounded this man within minutes of her arrival in Kezoban. But what she'd said was true; she was here primarily because he'd implied that she was the stallion's only hope.

The sound of insects from the darkness of the garden and the heady scents of the exotic flowers wrapped around her, making everything, from the man before her to the setting in which she'd just enjoyed the most delicious meal, even more romantic. She was tired from travelling yet her body fizzed with a new and strange fiery need.

'For that I am indebted to you. Tomorrow you will begin your work with Majeed and I am sure a spirited yet sympathetic woman such as you can help him.'

He moved towards her, his handsome face set in a firm mask of control, his dark eyes almost piercing hers. Was he teasing her? No, of course not. He was a powerful man, a ruler and used to getting what he wanted at all times.

'I'm looking forward to seeing the stallion. It will be an honour to work with such a majestic animal.' She tried to keep the conversation on the job, the reason she was here instead of allowing her mind to imagine he was looking at her with desire in his eyes.

'It will, no doubt, be a challenge.'

'I'm ready for a challenge.'

The smile which pulled at the corners of his lips did something to her, making her stomach flip as butterflies took flight. 'I shall walk you to your suite. This way.'

He gestured a path through the flora of the exquisite garden where small lights twinkled, giving it a magical appearance. She pushed aside her hesitancy and walked side by side with him, aware of his tall and strong body next to hers, just as she had been when they'd stood talking at the stables.

'Your gardens are so beautiful. I would never have expected it in the desert.' Again she talked to draw her attention away from the way he made her feel.

'I have spent many years researching irrigation in desert regions and now own a successful company doing just that.' The pride in his voice was clear and she looked at his profile, but when he turned to her she blushed, looking quickly away. 'Bringing water and better lives to my people is my passion.'

'Very impressive and interesting.'

'That pleases me.' His tone was more regal than she'd heard yet, reminding her just who this man was.

He opened a gate set beneath an arch of a white wall inlaid with intricate designs and stepped back to allow her through. 'These are the public palace gardens. You may walk in them whenever you wish.'

She walked beside him, more aware of him than she had ever been. He unsettled her with his raw masculinity and his overwhelming power, but more unnerving was the fact that she found him incredibly attractive.

She recognised the terraced area outside her suite but before she could say another word he stopped. 'I will bid you goodnight.'

She looked up at him, the intensity in his eyes sending a tremor of awareness surging through her. 'Thank you. For this evening.'

'The pleasure was all mine.'

A heavy silence fell over them, shrouding them in something profoundly powerful until she could hardly breathe. For one bizarre moment she thought he was going to kiss her and her body instinctively swayed towards his. Just in time she caught herself and stepped back. 'Goodnight.'

CHAPTER THREE

DESTINY DIDN'T SLEEP much that night. Her dreams were disturbed by the image of the man she'd spent the evening with. Zafir had infiltrated her mind, filling her thoughts with images of them together. She'd never behaved like this over a man before and, angry at her reaction, she got up early, going to sit on her private terrace, watching the sky turn from a dark orange to a bright and cloudless blue, bringing the warmth of a new day.

All she wanted was to begin her work with the Sheikh's stallion, but she would have to wait until she was escorted to the stables—or anywhere else within the palace. That much had been made clear to her on her arrival, making her feel more like a prisoner than a guest.

When a young boy knocked on her door and informed her he was to escort her to the stables it only reinforced that thought. She followed him through the bright white corridors of the palace, glimpsing the public part of the garden through the archways as she went, feeling the rising heat of the desert battle with the cool air within the palace.

Finally she reached the stables and the young boy

introduced her to the man in charge, but nothing could have prepared her for what she saw as she walked through another archway adorned with intricate metalwork. Beyond it she could see an almost endless row of stables on each side, all so elaborate it was hard to believe horses actually lived in them and a far cry from the stables her mother had started, which were now sadly neglected by her father. She used to think it was because he'd loved her mother so much that he couldn't face doing anything to them, but then she'd stumbled across her mother's diary and that myth had been shattered.

'Sheikh Al Asmari's stallion is stabled at the end,' the man said in almost perfect English, dragging her thoughts back from home. His plain white robes flared slightly as he walked towards the end of the long passageway, his feet almost silent on the sandy-coloured mosaic floor. He stopped and turned to her, caution and warning in his voice as he continued. 'The stallion will not leave the palace walls. Fear is in his eyes and mistrust in his soul. Many have tried to reach him, but none have succeeded.'

'He has not been outside these walls for almost a year?' Destiny knew a moment of panic as she realised this was a more serious problem than she'd been led to believe.

'Not since the Sheikh's young sister rode him out the night she died.'

'Then I have much work to do. I will need to spend time with him before I do anything else.' She was anxious to get started, wanting to see the horse for herself, needing to gain his trust. Only then could she begin to work with him and determine how long it would take, but already she wondered if the two months the Sheikh had stated would be adequate.

'This way.'

She followed the man to the end stable and couldn't help a gasp of admiration escape her. The stallion's black coat gleamed. He was as regal as his owner and easily had as much power and command surrounding him.

'I will groom him first.'

The man inclined his head in acknowledgement and a few moments later handed her several brushes. 'The bridle is hanging here.'

'Thank you.' She looked at the fine leather bridle adorned with bright coloured tassels, not sure any horse she'd worked with recently would tolerate such things on their bridles. Maybe Majeed wasn't so bad after all.

As the man walked away she entered the stable and stood, waiting for the stallion to accept her presence. His ears twitched as he inspected her from the corner of his stable, his head high and regal, his eyes wary.

'You're very handsome,' she said softly as she stood and waited for the stallion to relax. 'Almost as handsome as your master.'

Zafir's face came to mind in an image so clear it shocked her. She'd only seen him three times and already every last detail of those dark, attractive features was imprinted in her memory. If that wasn't a warning sign she was letting her imagination run wild, dragging her in too deep, she didn't know what was. The last thing she needed was the added complication of being attracted to the Sheikh.

* * *

Zafir had wanted to escort Destiny to the stables but had had to bow to protocol. She was here as his guest, a British woman employed to do a job and, as such, it wouldn't be right to be seen offering her extra favours. Especially now, when he was finally accepting his duty to marry and produce a future generation to rule Kezoban.

He entered the stables just in time to see Destiny go into Majeed's stable, apparently about to groom him. Not at all how others had approached the task. He frowned, then dismissed his doubts. He'd sought her out because of recommendation and he would have to accept her way of doing things—for now at least.

Silently he walked towards the stable and couldn't stem the satisfied smile as she spoke to the horse, complimenting both Majeed and him. It pleased him to know she was not as immune to him as she had led him to believe last night. It also notched up the simmering desire just being near her provoked.

As he'd walked her through the garden last night he'd known that if they were anywhere else but his palace he would have taken his attraction for her further. He would have kissed her. For the first time since he'd taken an oath to serve his people he wished such duties didn't exist, that he was free to explore whatever it was between them. As she'd looked up at him, her lovely face in partial darkness, he'd wanted to take her in his arms and savour her kiss, to hold her against him and become intoxicated by her sweet scent.

Had she known that? Had she wanted it too? Was that why she'd suddenly bolted last night as they'd stood by the terrace of her suite? He watched her now as she put out her hand, allowing Majeed to smell her. She didn't move, but the curious horse came to her. She touched his muzzle, then gently took hold of his head collar.

'Do you need any help?' He decided it would be best to make his presence known before he gave her and the horse a fright.

'How long have you been there?' She blushed and he knew she was worrying if he'd heard her earlier compliments to him and the horse.

'I have just arrived.'

She relaxed a little, then turned her attention to the horse. 'I will brush him for a while so that I can touch him all over, ensure he isn't unnerved by me. Then I will begin my work with him.'

Zafir found his thoughts wandering to how it would feel to be touched all over by her and for the first time in his life he was jealous of a horse. This woman seemed to bring out a magnitude of new emotions within him. What would be next?

He watched as she turned her back on him and began to brush Majeed's shiny black coat. She wore the traditional Western jodhpurs he'd seen her in when he'd called at the stables in England but, unlike then, she now wore a long shirt which covered her arms and the sexy bottom he'd studied briefly as he'd first watched her. She was bowing to his country's dress codes as much as her job would allow. For that he was grateful, but he couldn't help wondering what she'd look like in the silks women in his country wore. The thought intrigued him and he decided it would be something he would discover before she returned to England. He would give her a gift of the finest *abayas* and silks to wear.

'Very well, I will wait.'

She turned to look at him, her hand resting on Majeed's shoulder. 'For what?'

For a moment he couldn't speak. Nobody ever talked to him in that tone of voice. 'To see you work?' His tone was sharp with shock but the challenge in her eyes made him clench his jaw against further words.

'I don't work with an audience.'

'I am hardly an audience. I am the owner of this horse and, as the Sheikh of Kezoban, I expect to get what I want.' The audacity of the woman! How could she not know he would get just what he wanted and when he wanted it?

'Then we have a problem.'

'A problem?' Briefly he floundered, like a man stumbling down a large sand dune, his balance disrupted. 'I am not about to allow anyone to work with my horse without my knowledge of what is happening.'

She moved away from the horse, put down the brush and came to the door. 'Then it seems we have wasted one another's time.'

Had the world tipped on its axis? Had everything been turned upside down? He gave orders, not took them. He made demands, not met them.

She looked directly into his eyes, the shyness she'd displayed last night gone and in its place fierce determination.

'Can you help this horse?' He snapped the question out, his patience tested to the full and not just by her impertinence but by the way his body craved hers.

'Yes, I can, although it appears his master is in need

of some help too.' Her words were spoken in a low
tone with smooth flowing syllables, but the unrelent-
ing strength in them was unmistakable. Was it possible she knew how long he'd tortured himself with the
guilt of not being there for Tabinah, of not hearing her
pleas or understanding her unhappiness?

'You are not here to analyse me.' Maybe his pres-
ence here *would* affect the outcome. Was it possible
Majeed sensed his guilt? This was all too deep for him.
He didn't explore emotions—ever.

'When I work with a horse, I also invariably work
with the owner as well.' The slight rise of her delicate
brows gave her a superiority he found strangely attractive. Something else he didn't want to look too deeply
into. It was time to retreat. Time to gather his strength.

'Very well. I will meet you in my office this afternoon and I expect your verdict on what Majeed needs.'

'Thank you.' She didn't smile and he couldn't. She
had got the better of him, caught him totally off guard,
a sensation which both unsettled and excited him.

Later that afternoon Destiny waited to see Zafir. She'd
spent several hours with Majeed, wanting only to gain
his trust, because she could see beneath his fear. She
needed much more information about what had happened to change him so much. She sensed he was a
gentle creature who only wanted to please, which was
all the more reason to take things slowly.

The big problem now was how his master would
react to having the death of his sister all but investi-
gated by her.

'The Sheikh will see you now.' Zafir's aide approached and she followed him through the tall doors

she'd first entered on her arrival. Was that really only yesterday?

As she stood before him, his gaze slid down her in an imperious way that sent a shimmer of awareness all over her as if he'd actually touched her and she was glad of her continued choice of clothes which fitted in with his culture and, more importantly, covered as much of her as possible.

'You may leave us.' He spoke to his aide but kept his gaze firmly fixed on her and she blushed, wishing somebody would stay. He gestured to a large chair in front of his desk. 'Please, sit.'

She did as he bid her and sat on the gilded chair. The room was so large, with arches opening out onto yet more ornate gardens, but she couldn't focus on any of that now. Zafir took all her attention. She needed to keep her mind focused and to quash the heady feeling that rushed around her just from being in the same room as him. Was that why she'd been so adamant that he couldn't stay this morning? Because of the way he made her feel? Or was it the need to test his authority, to push his control back and gain some for herself?

'Now that you have had time with Majeed, what is your professional opinion?' His voice was deep with a firm edge to it that highlighted his accent. It also did things to her she had never known possible, like a tingle rushing down her spine and a heavy sensation deep within her.

'Majeed needs time and he needs to build his confidence by facing his fears. As he has not left the palace walls since the accident I suggest I work towards that ultimate goal.'

Zafir nodded as he sat in his large and very regal

chair. She had to keep her nerve, keep her mind from thinking of his dark skin, the trimmed beard that made him so incredibly attractive. But it was his eyes which unsettled her most. Their dark intensity reached within her, bringing out a woman she'd never wanted to be, one who desired a man, wanted him in a way that was as impossible as her being in his kingdom in the first place.

'I had anticipated that you would say that. Tomorrow morning we will ride out. I will take you to where Tabinah was found and endeavour to impart as much of the events as possible.' His tone was courteous, his words firm and distinct and she wondered if she'd just imagined the last few moments when something like attraction had sparked between them.

'That will be good. I understand it must be painful for you, but it is something…'

'Painful?' He cut her words off before she could finish the remainder of the sentence. 'Why would it be painful?'

'It must be hard after losing your sister because of the need to follow tradition.'

He stood up abruptly, his eyes eagle-sharp, almost pinning her to the spot. 'I had thought because of the way you have been dressing that you were acquainted with my culture.'

Destiny frowned, unsure what she'd said to have changed things so drastically, but she wouldn't allow him to intimidate her. She was here of her own free will and would leave if necessary. She stood up as quickly as he had, her chin defiantly lifted even though inside she was trembling. 'I'm sorry if my sympathy offends.'

'It does not offend. It is misplaced.' He tempered his

tone and walked around the desk towards her slowly as if he feared she might bolt through the archway at any moment and into the gardens.

'Misplaced?' The question came out as a cracked whisper and she could hardly stand, her limbs were so weak. Still he moved towards her, coming so close she could smell the desert on him and the heady, raw masculine scent of power.

'It was to have been a marriage of convenience. Love was not involved. Just as it will not be when I take a wife.' He looked down at her and she refused to break eye contact, watching him even though just being this close weakened her knees and made her pulse leap wildly. 'Marriage is a contract, nothing more.'

'But what about love?' She couldn't help the question slipping from her lips and as she spoke his gaze flicked lower, as if watching her lips move, and she had to fight hard against the urge to bite down on her bottom lip. What was this man doing to her?

'Love is a concept I have not allowed in my life. Desire, however, is.' She could see it in his eyes, feel it with every pore of her skin. At that moment he desired her. Light-headed and shocked, she backed away from him, bumping into the chair she'd just leapt from.

'That is not something I know.' Why did her voice sound so husky?

'You have not desired something?' He was playing with her; she was sure of that. Was it punishment for speaking out of turn?

'Yes, of course I've desired things.' She let out a long breath. For a moment she'd thought he meant a man.

'Someone?'

She looked at him, knowing that right now she desired him. What had he done to her? He was a powerful Sheikh, a man used to getting what he wanted and probably had a harem of women tucked away in his palace somewhere. She had to stop this. She was getting in way too deep. If she wasn't careful, she would go down the same sorry road as her mother, falling for a man who could never love her.

'No. I have never desired anyone and neither do I intend to.'

'So if I touched your face with my fingertips you wouldn't tremble with desire and need for me.'

He reached out his hand and before he could touch her she knocked his arm away, glaring angrily at him. 'I am not here to become one of your harem. I am here to work with your stallion. Nothing more.'

He narrowed his eyes and she knew she'd insulted him. Was it because she'd touched him or because she hadn't fallen into a heap at his feet, begging him to make love to her?

'I do not have a harem of any size and I will be faithful to my wife from the day we are married. No woman has come close to threatening that ideal before today.' He turned on his heel, his robes flowing out wildly, and went to stand by the archway, the sunlight of the afternoon framing him.

He looked vulnerable and she swallowed down hard, finally able to breathe properly now that he'd stepped away. Last night she'd believed she'd been mistaken when she'd thought he'd been about to kiss her; now she wasn't sure. Was she doing something wrong? Giving him the wrong message? She was a naive virgin who'd barely shared a kiss with a man and this particular man was so overwhelmingly powerful she couldn't understand, let alone control, the way he made her feel.

'You should leave.' He didn't look at her and the rigid set of his back made his disapproval all too evident but she wasn't about to argue with him again.

She needed to get away, to calm herself and work out what was going on between them. Every time they met it became more intense, harder to ignore. Whatever *it* was.

She turned and walked to the door, about to reach for the large gold handle when she heard his voice again. Deep and soft.

'Destiny.'

She turned to him, not liking the way her heart lurched at the sight of him. Even across the vastness of his cool marbled office, she could feel his vulnerability, as if every barrier he'd ever used as a weapon was briefly down, exposing the real man.

'Yes?' she said stiffly, not willing to be fooled by his soft tone.

He frowned and regarded her suspiciously. 'Be ready by dawn.'

'Ready?' Her heart went into freefall. Ready for what?

'To ride out. We leave before the sun rises too high.'

His eyes locked with hers across the room and she couldn't break the contact, couldn't look away. Instead she nodded, her breath coming hard and fast. Finally she dropped her gaze and turned to pull open the door quickly, her haste to escape whatever spell he was casting on her making her clumsy.

How could she want a man such as this hard and dominating Sheikh? She couldn't answer that, but she did know she would have to keep her emotions much more firmly under control. He was too much like the man who'd broken her mother's heart and dominated her life ever since. So why did she yearn for his touch, his kiss?

CHAPTER FOUR

ZAFIR HAD BEEN up long before the first tendrils of dawn had shown themselves in the sky and now he waited impatiently at the stables. He'd wished he could simply go to Destiny's suite and escort her himself, but if he wanted to avoid scandal and protect her reputation, protocol had to be followed. He was the Sheikh and she was an unmarried woman. Their dinner on her first night had pushed those boundaries—and he'd always pushed boundaries—but with his staff waiting on them he'd considered them enough of a chaperone.

Yesterday he'd impulsively banished all his staff from his office, probably giving rise to speculation about why Destiny was here in Kezoban. He knew well enough how the tongues of gossip could spread rumours through his palace, yet now he was about to ride out into the desert alone with her because he didn't want her to hear the more elaborate tales connected with his sister's death. The only way to ensure that was to take her into the desert himself, tell her only what she needed to know. But still he questioned if he'd lost all sense of reason.

In a way he was not yet able to understand, Destiny scrambled his usual cool and rational thoughts.

He had a business to oversee as well as a kingdom to rule, duties and expectations to meet, and none of them involved the brown-eyed woman who had haunted his sleep, making him want things he could no longer have from the first moment he'd seen her working the chestnut mare in England.

He strode to the stables, knowing that soon he would be able to escape the confines of the palace—for a short while at least. Riding across the desert sands, following the edge of the river that was the lifeblood of his kingdom was the only time he ever felt truly free to be himself.

He'd never allowed anyone to accompany him before. Did it signify something deeper that he wanted Destiny to share such an intimate moment with him? Could it be more than attraction which kept pulling them ever closer to each other? He had to push aside the temptation to make it something more, even though he wanted to explore it until it fizzled out, as desire always did.

Movement behind him made him turn as he reached the ornate archway to the stables. Destiny was being escorted towards him and, as he watched her gracefully walk, he couldn't drag his gaze from her. She was beautiful and mesmerising.

A whispered curse slipped from his lips. What was he? A youth who'd never touched a woman before? It was so far from the truth, but right now he could be exactly that.

'Good morning.' She smiled at him as he dismissed her escort. 'I'm looking forward to this. Riding in the desert, I mean.'

Satisfaction slipped over him as she blushed, her

last words all but highlighting that she'd been looking forward not just to riding in the desert, but being with him. Again thoughts of a dalliance with this English woman rushed through his mind. He'd been committed to his duty from the first day he'd become the ruler of Kezoban, working hard and leaving behind a life of playing, one which had been filled with many beautiful women. He'd been faithful and true to his people, just as he would be to his new bride. But as yet he had not selected a bride from those chosen for him, and neither did he want to when all he could think of was Destiny Richards.

'As am I.' He looked down at her as colour stained her pale skin. 'It will be an honour to show you some of my country. The horses are ready.'

He turned and walked briskly to the end of the row of stables, where the tall arched doors were already wide open, as were those in the palace walls, showing the gold of the desert sand beyond. As always, pride swelled in his chest to think this was his country and that the people in it looked to him for leadership.

'I will need to see where the incident with Majeed and your sister happened.' Her voice was hesitant as she spoke of Tabinah.

'We shall go there first and after we can relax and enjoy the ride. I want you to experience my country at its best before the heat becomes too fierce for your fair skin.' As he spoke her eyes met and held his, their warm brown reminding him not for the first time of deeply polished mahogany.

He wanted to kiss her, to taste her on his lips and feel her against his body. He hadn't wanted a woman like this for many years—ever.

'We should go.' The cracked whisper of her voice was almost his undoing and he had to ignore the burning need rushing through him more fiercely than a desert storm.

'Yes.' He snapped the word out, opening the stable door of his finest grey Arab mare. 'This is Halima. Her name means "gentle" and I have selected her for her kind nature entwined with a courageous spirit.'

He wanted to add that was how he saw her and that maybe her name meant she had been fated to come into his life, but her obvious pleasure in the mare stemmed the words.

She reached out her hand to the mare, which sniffed curiously at the long slender fingers and Zafir couldn't drag his gaze from them. 'You are beautiful.' Her voice was soft and full of wonder as she spoke, sending a rush of heat hurtling through him.

'A beautiful horse for a beautiful woman.' The words were out before he could stop himself. Was it so wrong to express his thoughts? The expression on her face warned that now was not the time.

'You shouldn't say that.' Destiny's face heated as he continued to watch her with those midnight black eyes while she tightened her large scarf around her head. She didn't want her stomach to flip with anticipation, or her pulse to race with something close to desire for this man. She didn't want to find such a dominating and controlling man attractive. She hadn't hidden away from men's attention only to fall under this man's spell. How could she when she'd lived all her life under her father's iron rule?

'But I have and now I cannot take it back.'

Suddenly he moved to the next stable, leaving her holding the reins of her mare as he walked out a stunning grey stallion whose coat was flecked with brown and looked almost as commanding as Zafir.

She didn't say anything but led out her horse and mounted, a thrill of excitement rushing through her at the new experience of riding in the desert. Or was it simply the thrill of riding out with Zafir which excited her? That was a question she couldn't even think about.

When she looked at him, mounted on the stallion, which was restlessly all but dancing on the spot, her breath caught in her throat. Nothing could have prepared her for the image he created—one of power and command. He was devastatingly attractive and, for her sins, she wished he really had noticed her, that his compliment had been real, that he felt every spark too.

Enough, she reprimanded herself. She wasn't here to fall for a man, let alone one as commanding as Sheikh Zafir Al Asmari. She was here to work, to secure her new life, her future. 'Shall we?'

A smile twitched at the corners of his lips, then he pushed his mount on and she nudged her mare forward, following him into the outer region of the palace. The large cream stone walls loomed ahead of them and already the sun was warm.

As they approached the imposing and fortified doors in the walls, another rider came to join them and Zafir turned in the saddle, the fast flow of Arabic words sounding strange as he addressed the other man, who she recognised as one of his aides. Their words seemed heated and as her mare shifted excitedly on the spot she couldn't mistake the anger emanating from Zafir as his aide returned to the stables.

Before she could gather her thoughts Zafir turned to her. 'Come.' Seconds later, in a cloud of dusty sand, Zafir and the stallion were surging forward into the desert, her mare so eager for a gallop she could hardly hold her back.

It was exhilarating. Hooves thundered on the ground and the wind was warm on her face. Just ahead of her Zafir began to slow his pace and gradually the horses dropped back to a walk. Had he been so angry after speaking with his aide he'd needed to take off as if the devil were after him or did he always push his horses so hard?

'What was wrong just now?' she asked tentatively, wondering if she'd done something wrong by riding out with him. But it had been his idea.

'My aide is aggrieved we are out unchaperoned.' The harsh tone of his voice told her he did not share that view.

'Is my presence a problem for you?' She stroked the silky neck of the mare, guessing that her presence in Kezoban was probably creating some difficulties for him, even if he was the Sheikh.

'For me no, but for you, yes.' His profile was regal and stern as she glanced over at him. His back was tall and straight as he sat on the horse and she knew it was something he'd done since he was young. He was a natural horseman.

'For me? Why?'

'I am unmarried. As are you. Being alone with you goes against my culture. My aide reminded me of my duty to marry before the end of this year.'

She tried to stem the flow of disappointment his words brought. Of course she was a problem and of course they shouldn't be alone together. 'So being here *is* a problem for you?'

'No.' He turned to her, his dark eyes fierce as his horse stood level with hers, giving her little escape from the intensity in his eyes. 'It is not a problem for me. I want you here. You are what Majeed needs—and you are what I need.'

She couldn't say anything for a moment as the horses walked side by side and his eyes remained locked with hers. Something arced between them, more powerful than the sun's rays bouncing off the nearby water, lending the whole conversation a different meaning. Shock raced like lightning down her spine because right now she wanted to be the person he needed.

'I would like to talk more on this, but first we should deal with your request to know about the night Tabinah rode Majeed out here and met her death.' The strong determination in his voice couldn't conceal his pain at the loss of his sister so tragically.

Zafir halted his horse and dismounted and she followed suit, but as she did so she found herself falling into his waiting arms. He didn't let her go, pulling her close against him, and being held like that sent a spark hurtling through her. What was she thinking? This was where his sister had died. She shouldn't be wanting more when just being here would be painful for him. Quickly she moved free of his hold and for a moment thought she saw a flash of pain and guilt rush across his face, but as it disappeared behind his mask of control she wondered if she'd imagined it.

'This is where it is believed Tabinah began to make her way towards the rocky path over the mountains.' He paused for a moment and she didn't say anything, aware of just how difficult this must be for him. 'Her destination was on the other side.'

'So you knew where she was going?' He said nothing, but nodded his acknowledgement. She wanted to ask why Tabinah had planned to go over the mountains, but something kept the question a silent thought. She recalled him telling her that Tabinah had loved another man, one he didn't consider suitable. Her heart lurched for him. Maybe this proud and powerful man was able to feel grief. He just kept it deeply hidden. 'Do you know what happened?'

'There are many venomous snakes lurking in the shade of the rocks—they shelter beneath them at nightfall. We believe Majeed disturbed one, reared and Tabinah fell. The bite of the snake killed her, not the fall.'

'Majeed must feel so guilty.' She spoke in a soft whisper, more to herself than Zafir.

'Is it possible for a horse to feel guilty?'

'That is why he will not venture out beyond the palace walls. He is carrying guilt and fear over what happened. From what I have seen so far, he only wants to please and he knows he has displeased so won't come here again for fear of retribution.'

'I'm not sure I agree,' he said as he agilely flung himself back on his horse, thankfully putting more distance between them, giving her racing heart a chance to slow. 'Now you have the information you need, we ride.'

Destiny mounted her mare again and followed Zafir as his stallion began to trot away from the mountains that his sister had been trying to reach and back towards the sand of the desert. Thankfully, the mood lightened as the pace became fast and she couldn't help but laugh with delight when the wind snatched at her scarf, pulling it from her head and allowing her hair to be blown back behind her.

Zafir turned and glanced at her, but didn't slow as she thought he would. Instead he pushed the stallion on, increasing the pace and her exhilaration.

Finally Destiny saw Zafir slow his pace and eased her willing mare back. As she slowed she was able to look about her, seeing nothing but sand. It was strangely beautiful, shades of gold sculpted by the winds, and it felt right being here. Even the sun's ever increasing height didn't worry her. It would be hot very soon, of that she was sure, but she trusted Zafir; he wouldn't bring them here if they couldn't make it back before the sun scorched everything.

'This is where I ride to every morning.' His heavily accented words filtered through her thoughts. She looked about her. The sun was climbing ever higher and the wind was warm and very dry. As far as she could see was sand. Not another soul, just the two of them, and it felt strangely intimate. Exciting.

'It's beautiful,' she breathed as the horses walked on, slowly climbing before reaching the top of a dune. She looked out across a sea of sand and in the distance saw the range of mountains. 'It's more than beautiful—it's utterly gorgeous.'

'As are you.' His words were firm, but huskiness accentuated his accent, making her heart skip a beat.

Destiny looked across at him, the grey stallion prancing on the spot, but still Zafir kept his gaze fixed on her. He looked so regal in his desert robes, the wind blowing the headdress which concealed his dark hair.

Heat which had nothing to do with the sun sizzled down her spine.

In a total abandonment she'd never experienced before, she knew she wanted to be kissed by him, to be held in his strong arms. Her body was on fire for him. She wanted to be claimed by this man, wanted him to make her completely his. She wanted him and, more importantly, he wanted her. She should have seen it all along. The attraction which had sparked to life the first time they'd met was too strong to be ignored. No amount of professionalism or contrived distance could deny it.

This was a man fate had sent her way. A man so wild and exotic he could have been conjured up by her imagination. She had never hungered after passion and certainly not with a man such as Zafir but now that she had met him she knew it would only ever be him she'd want.

'I want you, Zafir.' She could scarcely believe she'd said the words. Her heart was pounding so fast in her chest, but she'd had to say it, had to tell him. Here, away from the palace, he seemed different, more relaxed, more like the man she'd thought had been about to kiss her that very first night. She too felt different out here, as if she'd uncovered a hidden part of her as they'd galloped across the sands, then discarded her usual caution, losing it to the warm winds, making her a different woman.

Zafir's horse whipped round, pawing the sand, eager to be off, but he soothed the agitation with words she didn't understand, words that sounded like poetry to her.

'I can't offer you what you're looking for, Destiny,'

he said, his voice almost harsh as he struggled with the prancing stallion.

Destiny's mare instantly picked up the excited vibes from the stallion and turned, leaving her facing Zafir, able to look into the dark swirling depths of his eyes.

'What am I looking for, Zafir?' she asked as the mare spun round again. Destiny held the reins firm, her body moving with each excited step the mare took and waited for his answer.

'I can't give you forever. I can't even promise you happiness, but I can promise you a night like no other.'

Deep down she'd known that all along, known that he was so far removed from her world that they would never have any kind of future together. But that hadn't stopped her wanting him from that very first moment she'd seen him at her stables—even if she hadn't recognised it then.

Happy-ever-after would be nice. A dream come true. But dreams didn't come true—her mother was testament to that—and before her now was a man offering her a taste of such a dream. A taste she intended to sample to the full. She wanted to know what passion and desire felt like before she returned to a fresh start in England.

'I hope you keep your promises, Your Highness,' she teased, feeling a recklessness she'd never known around a man before, and launched the mare into a gallop. Behind her she heard Zafir's mount as it whinnied with excitement, then the thundering of its hooves as the distance closed between them.

She laughed out loud, the wind snatching the sound away. She was totally free. The glint of passion she'd glimpsed in Zafir's eyes before she'd raced off hummed inside her as excitement and anticipation grew. She would be brave and sample the dream of happiness and forever, even if it was only for one night.

Zafir was relieved and angered as he saw his palace coming into view. The horses were hot and tired but still he wished he could have stayed out in the desert with Destiny all day. She made him feel alive, made him long to be carefree and wild, something he hadn't felt for many years, but once back within the confines of the palace he'd have to school his emotions, behave in the manner of the ruler he was.

His promise of one night would be all he could give her. She was not of his world and soon, too soon, he was going to have to select a bride—to provide the heirs his position demanded. His wife needed to be a woman able to deal with the harshness of not only desert life, but life married to the ruler of Kezoban. She needed to be someone his people could relate to, someone they could take to their hearts.

Destiny's dark hair was flowing behind her, the scarf she'd worn blowing in the wind. He deliberately held his mount back, enabling him to watch her, his eyes drawn to the firmness of her thighs as she pushed her mare on and the tantalising outline of her bottom as she leant forward in the saddle. She was gorgeous, beautiful and so full of life—exactly the kind of woman he wished he could have if his position as ruler of Kezoban didn't demand otherwise.

Excitement fizzed through him, making him ache with unquenched passion as he recalled her words. She wanted him, seeming to accept they had little or no future, even teasing him as she'd headed back across the sand. In that moment he knew he had to have her, had to make her his. She might be off limits but she would be his for one night.

Stable boys greeted them as they made their way back within the safety of palace walls. He couldn't resist another look at Destiny. Her cheeks were flushed from exertion, her eyes bright and alive. He wanted her so badly that if he was to avoid carrying her off to his bed right this minute he'd have to throw himself into his work.

'Thank you,' she breathed after dismounting, suddenly close to him. Too close.

'For what?' he asked, suspicion furrowing his brow, unaware he had done anything that required her thanks.

'For just now—it was wonderful. I haven't enjoyed a good gallop since Ellie was sold.'

'Who is Ellie?' He watched as she looked down at her hands as if trying to hide her emotions.

'My horse. Or she was until my father forced me to sell her. He couldn't accept the time I spent with Ellie.'

He sensed there was more, knew that, like him, she was hiding a part of herself. 'I'm sorry, but you may, of course, ride the mare any time.'

Around him Zafir was aware of the bustle of activity as the horses were led away. Destiny placed her hand on his arm as soon as they were alone. 'Thank you, for that and…' She paused, as if wondering if she should give voice to her thoughts.

Out there in the desert she'd been completely honest with him and, going against his better judgement, he'd been honest with her.

'For bringing me here and enabling me to have the chance of making a new start when I return home.' She

looked up at him as she continued, directly into his
eyes, and he saw a conflict of emotions racing across
them before she lowered her lashes, shutting him out.

'I am honoured to have you here.' His voice was
a cracked whisper as he closed the distance between
them so that they were almost touching. His heart
began to thump harder as he slowly and very gently
held her face, his thumbs caressing her cheekbones.
Very slowly, so slowly it was almost painful, he lowered his head until his lips brushed hers.

Heat skittered around Destiny's body with alarming
speed, a soft sigh escaping her lips, only to be caught
by his kiss. His stubble grazed her skin and her senses
whirled as she inhaled his scent—bergamot, fresh and
clean but with a hint of the desert.

Everything about the kiss felt so right, as did being
this close to the heated hardness of his body. She ached
to pull him closer, to wind her arms around his neck
and slide her fingers into his hair. She wasn't sure how
she even knew what to do. She was simply following
her body's instinct.

'You smell good,' he whispered against her lips and
her stomach flipped over, making her knees so weak
she wondered if they'd be able to keep her upright. 'It
is a change to find a woman who is happy not to be
permanently doused in perfume, living life to the full.'

Destiny pulled back and looked sceptically up into
his face. 'I'm not sure the last bit is a compliment or
not,' she teased.

'Your sweet scent, so distinctly you, cannot be
doused even as it mixes with leather and horse,' he said
with a hint of a smile on his lips. Those heady words

said by any other man would have sounded strange, but from Zafir, the man she desired with increasing need, they were like dynamite. The explosion of desire within her sealed her fate. She was already his.

'And that is good?' she teased him, emboldened by the fact that he had even noticed such details.

'Oh, it's good.' He feathered a kiss across her brow. 'I admire a woman who doesn't feel she has to be dressed in finery and decked in jewels. You're so different from any woman I've met before.'

Destiny couldn't help the image of what his past lovers must have been like coming into her head. Had any of them been the kind of woman he loved? Or was he referring to his sister? Maybe if she knew more of Tabinah she could not only help Majeed but satisfy her curiosity.

Finally that curiosity got the better of her and the words slipped from her lips before she could think of the consequences. 'What was Tabinah like?'

Zafir's body went cold and rigid against her instantly and she regretted her impetuous words. Surely there had been another way of asking the question. His arms dropped away from her and he stepped back.

'What Tabinah was like has no relevance to you or your work here.' The words snapped angrily from him and she cursed her stupid timing, but felt angered by his inability to open up to her, to allow her in. 'You have seen where the incident took place, where my sister was found. You do not need to know any more.'

'That is where you are wrong.' She said the words a little too quickly and moved farther away from him. If distance was what he craved, distance he'd get. 'I need to know so much more than you are willing to tell if you want me to help Majeed.'

'You do not, I repeat, do not need to know about my sister or my relationship with her.'

His eyes glittered as if the sun were shining on thousands of tiny diamonds. It should have served as a warning to her but she didn't see it, didn't want to see it.

'I'm making a connection with Majeed. He's letting me close, giving me his trust and it's a shame his master can't do the same.'

Before he could answer she marched from the stables and back towards the courtyard and the long wide corridor which led to the palace, not bothering to wait for her escort. Anger boiled inside her. How could he bring her here to help a horse he had no intention of helping himself?

Once inside her room she shut the door, leant her back against it and only then allowed her nerves full rein. Her body shook as if she was cold, her legs so weak she couldn't stand any longer and she slid down the door. It was not the way she'd spoken to the Sheikh, the ruler, or even the fact that he'd held her so tenderly, kissing her gently yet with barely concealed passion. It was the way she'd responded. From that first teasing moment in the desert when she'd all but begged him to make her his lover, to the way she'd allowed his mouth to claim hers.

She was doing exactly what she knew she shouldn't, what could only bring heartache and trouble. But she couldn't stop herself, couldn't help the fire that burned deep within her just thinking of him.

She was falling for the Sheikh, the devil of the desert.

CHAPTER FIVE

FOR THE LAST two weeks Zafir had adhered to all the rules he'd mentioned at the beginning of their ride that morning in the desert, although that day they had both briefly thrown those rules to the wind as the horses had raced homeward. Destiny could still feel his lips on hers, still wanted so much more, but, just as he obviously didn't wish to, she wouldn't give into the attraction. Since their ride he'd been the perfect gentleman when they'd met and had ensured they had company at all times.

Zafir had allocated her a maid and she was certain it was to ensure they didn't find themselves alone again. Although the older woman had seemed initially in awe of her, she had found a good friend in Mina. Soon after had come the generous gifts of gorgeous silk *abayas* and other garments worn by the women of Zafir's kingdom and she kept telling herself he just wanted her to feel comfortable, to fit in and be part of life in the palace.

Each time she'd met with Zafir in his office to report on her progress with Majeed, he'd had at least one of his aides present, making it clear he'd inadvertently crossed boundaries and had spent the last two weeks erecting higher barriers between them.

In the thrill of the moment that morning, flirtation had taken over and she'd recklessly agreed to just one night. She'd agonised over how she would tell him she'd never spent one moment intimately with a man, let alone a night. But that now appeared a needless worry. Not once had he done anything to make her think he was still serious about spending a night with her.

For the last few hours Destiny had been at the stables with Majeed and she was shocked at the dishevelled state in her reflection as she passed the ornate gilt mirror in her suite. Her hair was wild, looking as if she hadn't been near a hairdresser for years, not weeks. Her face was streaked with dust after working with Majeed in the school; the long white blouse she'd worn for modesty was now grimy and dirty.

She'd looked as dishevelled the morning she and Zafir had returned from their ride, but he had seen past that then. She'd really believed he'd seen her for who she really was, that he'd wanted her in the way she'd wanted him. Doubts assailed her as she unbuttoned her blouse, dropping it to the marble floor and heading for the shower. She turned on the jets of warm water, discarded the remainder of her clothes and stepped under the soothing warmth of the water.

As she was dressing in one of the cool outfits Zafir had provided for her to wear when she wasn't working, Mina knocked and entered. The big smile on the woman's face showed nothing but approval for her choice of pale blue silks adorned with gold. 'His Highness has requested that you join him for an outing to the town.'

Destiny's heart jolted before hammering out a

steady beat. Zafir wanted to take her out. It would be a welcome change from working each day and, feeling like an excited child, she clasped her hands together in front of her chest in a way that had a lot more to do with the man who was taking her out rather than the outing itself.

'Do I need to change?' she asked Mina, wondering where they were going and if what she now wore was suitable.

'You have chosen well. I will be happy to be seen with you,' Mina said as she moved forward and fussed with the vibrant blue silk.

'Be seen with me?' she queried, the rush of anticipation at spending time with Zafir becoming clouded.

'It wouldn't be good for His Highness to be seen alone with you.' Mina stood back to survey her efforts, unaware of the confusion that ran riot inside Destiny's head. 'Now, if you are ready, we shall go.'

She followed Mina along the cool corridors, trying all the while to hide her disappointment that she and Zafir were to be accompanied. She wondered if this chaperone was intended for her sake or his. Then all her thoughts jumbled as they entered a large room where Zafir, deep in conversation with his aide, was dressed in robes befitting a king. The white robes, layered with a fine gold cloak, accentuated his potent masculinity and undoubted power, making her stomach knot and a heavy throb of desire pulse deep inside her.

She couldn't take her eyes from him. And from the fire within his, the question of their one night together still lingered tantalisingly between them. Had he kept his distance purposefully in an attempt to make her want him more?

Mina stepped into the background, as did his aide, and suddenly it was just the two of them again. His steady gaze held hers, forcing her heart rate to accelerate wildly. She'd never known such an attraction before and the hot desire in his midnight black eyes was almost too much.

A smile pulled at the corners of his mouth, as if he'd read her thoughts, heard her secret appraisal of him. 'I thought you would like to sample life in our city,' he said as he moved farther away from the other man, coming to join her. His gaze slid down her body and she tingled all over as if he'd actually touched her, a ragged breath escaping her as she tried to speak.

'Thank you, Your Highness.' She managed to sound demure even though her rampaging emotions were making her want things she shouldn't. If they were to be chaperoned she'd better conform to the expected etiquette when addressing him in public. 'It will be nice to see more of your country before I return to England.'

He quirked a heavy dark brow at her words, his gaze holding hers for just a little too long, causing his aide to cough politely behind him. 'I shall be honoured to show you.' Then he bowed his head quickly and turned, his white robe swirling around him, the gold cloak shimmering in the light.

It all felt surreal and Destiny wondered if she was dreaming as they were ushered out into the heat of the day and into a waiting car. She looked around as the door closed them inside the luxury of his car. She and Zafir were alone. No aide and no chaperone.

'They will follow in the car behind,' he offered as if he'd read her thoughts.

She drank in the image he created as he sat tall and proud, even though he couldn't be seen through the tinted windows. Her body ached for him, craved his touch, his kiss. The weeks since that snatched moment in the stables had done little to quell the throb of desire whenever he was near. The memory of his kiss still burned in her mind and on her lips.

He leant closer and for one moment she thought he was going to kiss her again. Instead he said softly and so quietly only she could hear, 'Do you remember what we spoke of the morning we rode out?'

She'd thought of nothing else. It was what she wanted. Did this mean it was a serious proposition instead of fun flirtation?

When she didn't respond to his question he leant a little closer. 'Do you still want me, Destiny?'

'Yes.' The cracked whisper which came from her sounded unreal and so unnatural.

He smiled a satisfied and very sexy smile, sending her senses into overdrive, but how their one night was ever going to happen, when either his aide or Mina was present each time they met, she didn't know.

He reached out and stroked the back of his fingers down her cheek, forcing her lashes to close and a soft sigh to escape her lips. He was speaking, she realised, but in Arabic, which served only to highlight how different their lives were. She pulled back and for a moment their gazes locked, the challenge and desire in his clear.

'Will Royal protocol be happy with us travelling together?' she couldn't resist teasing as she sat back, feigning indifference to him.

RACHAEL THOMAS 73

* * *

'It is only a short drive.' Zafir's gaze wandered over her as she looked out of the window, anywhere but at him, it would seem. The heat created moments ago by her whispered admission that she wanted him was only intensified by her apparent lack of interest in him. She was aloof, so superior and a far cry from the passionate woman he'd held far too briefly in his arms two weeks ago. Since then he hadn't been able to stop thinking of her, wanting so much more than a kiss. 'And we do have a driver, although he does not understand English.'

'So why the escort? Why any of this?' She turned and faced him and he fought hard to remain straight and upright in his seat, resisting the urge to reach for her and pull her close. He wanted to feel her body against his, touch her, taste her and kiss her in a way he'd never done with any woman before.

'I thought you'd want to see more than just the palace. Having an escort is not only what my people would expect, but also for your own good. I do not wish to tarnish your reputation in any way.' Zafir felt her gaze travel over him, leaving a trail of fire that set light to the desire he'd tried to deny since he'd first seen her working the horse at the stables in England.

'Oh,' she whispered, as if aware of how she was affecting him. 'I'm sorry if I've caused you a problem.'

The only problem she'd caused him was awakening his long ignored libido, leaving him unfulfilled and as ravenous as a man breaking a fast. And this was a problem he intended to redress fully once the hours of darkness had fallen. He'd tried to dismiss whatever it was between them but he couldn't ignore her or his need for her any longer.

Tonight she would be his.

He knew he shouldn't want her, but he couldn't resist her any longer. In a matter of weeks he would be expected to announce his engagement, but still he hadn't made any final decision, despite being urged by his aides to do so. He pushed the unsavoury thought of marriage aside, his senses clamouring for the satisfaction he knew only Destiny could give.

'It is not a problem, just our way.' He watched as she looked down at her hands clasped tightly in her lap, something he'd seen her do on that first night at the palace. It made her appear vulnerable, a trait he had no intention of looking for in his future wife, but one he found himself drawn to in Destiny. He wanted to look after her, protect her from hurt and even, he conceded, protect her from himself—and right now that was what she needed most.

The car stopped at the hotel he'd planned on and as the door opened he couldn't help but find pleasure in her smile. The noisy bustle of the streets filled the car and he watched as she got out carefully, mindful of her new garments.

'Come,' he ordered. 'We shall walk to the market before taking some light refreshment.'

'You actually walk in the street?' The incredulity in her voice forced him to stem his laughter.

'How else am I to show you my city?'

'But I hadn't thought… I mean…' She floundered and he wanted to touch her, to ease her discomfort. But in public, protocol *had* to be followed. No matter what.

'That I wouldn't do such a thing? They are my people and I am privileged to walk among them. It is expected.'

As they walked on, her attention was captured, or so she'd have him believe, by the hustle of the town as they made their way through the busy streets. He smiled as she looked from side to side, desperate not to miss anything. Spending a few hours with her would be enjoyable, even if they did have the constant shadow of Mina over them. It would also heighten the anticipation of the night he had every intention of spending with her.

Negotiating the busy streets proved to be somewhat of a distraction, but Zafir had the constant urge to keep Destiny safe, to maintain contact. The need to touch her was so great it was driving him crazy and with his hand almost permanently moving to the small of her back before being quickly withdrawn, he showed her the wonders of his city while they mingled with the crowds.

'This is such a wonderful place.' She turned her face up to his and smiled—a wide carefree smile that he'd not witnessed on her lips until that moment. 'The colours, the smells, the noise. It's just wonderful.'

He looked down at her face; excitement was sparkling in her eyes. She was so beautiful, so vibrant that she cast everything around her into shadow. Did she have any idea what she did to him? He wanted her so badly, but what if he hurt her, made her unhappy or, worse, let her down as he'd let Tabinah down? What if by being with him, even now, here in the market, she would be exposing herself to future unhappiness?

'Zafir?' she queried. 'What's the matter? You look like you've seen a ghost.'

Perhaps I have. The thought ploughed into him like

a runaway horse. *Perhaps I'm seeing the ghost of the man I could have been if we were both different people.*

'No, everything is fine. I'm pleased you are enjoying yourself. You've been working hard with Majeed.'

She smiled shyly at him before looking away. Was she so unused to praise? He stifled a deep sigh, acknowledging but not accepting he was not what she needed. There might be chemistry between them, but she needed more than that, much more. Something he couldn't give. Something he didn't want to give.

'When you are ready we will have our refreshment before returning to the palace. It's hotter than I'd anticipated.' The words were all but snapped from him as he tried to prevent the guilt he felt at letting Tabinah down from surfacing. Destiny didn't need to know all the sorry details of his last exchange of words with his sister, despite what she thought, because if she did she'd never see him the same way again.

'You're right,' Destiny said as she turned to look at some bright red silk, desperate to hide her disappointment at his withdrawal from her. She'd felt him retreat, felt the hot passionate man she'd glimpsed in the back of the car fade away. His eyes had grown hard and cold, his body had tensed as the totally-in-control ruler had returned. 'It's hot. I'm ready to return to the palace now, please.'

Moments later she was once again in the back of his car as it made its way out of the busy streets before heading back to the palace. Beside her, Zafir was a dark brooding presence.

'I have work to attend to now.' He kept his gaze focused ahead, as if he couldn't even bear to look at her. Had she misread the signals yet again?

The car stopped outside the palace and she knew she had to say something. 'Zafir?' She hated the question in her voice, but it caught his attention and he turned to look at her as his door was opened. She lost her nerve as his dark eyes locked with hers. 'Thank you for a nice afternoon.'

No, not that. In her mind she screamed the words as he appeared to digest what she'd said without a trace of emotion on his regal face.

'My pleasure,' he said sharply and left the confines of the car, speaking rapidly to his staff, his words fast and flowing.

Then her own door opened and she got out into the heat of the afternoon, glad to walk into the shade of the palace and even more pleased when she was finally alone in her room.

More bereft than she'd ever felt, although she missed her sister, as always, her thoughts went to her mother. What would she have suggested she do? Destiny dug her teeth into her bottom lip in a bid to stop the tears falling. She wouldn't let Zafir's sudden coldness shatter her into pieces. She was stronger than that. Life had made her stronger.

In an attempt to feel close to her mother, she opened her wardrobe and pulled out her bag, then the small box she kept her mother's diary in. Just as she always did, she smoothed her fingers over the top of the box, then opened it and touched the diary which lay within. It was the last true connection she had with who she really was and she'd been so glad she'd found it hidden away at the back of her mother's wardrobe.

She turned to the usual page she read and traced her finger over the flowing words.

I thought I'd found my forever love in the man I married and now I don't know what to do. We have a beautiful daughter who was my destiny and another child on the way, but his affection is growing cold and I feel now his love for me never existed.

Carefully, Destiny closed the diary and placed it back in the box and buried it in her bag once more. Her mother had wanted love but never really found it. Dwelling on the past wasn't going to help her now. Sleep, however, would, she decided, and lay on the bed, allowing its softness to cradle her, to soothe her as she closed her eyes.

When sleep came it was filled with images of the Sheikh she'd lost her heart to, the man she wanted above all others—the man she couldn't have.

It was dark when she woke, only a soft glow from a small lamp illuminating the room. Destiny sat up, feeling more emotionally drained than she had before she'd slept. On the table she noticed covered dishes and realised Mina must have been in with her meal and left her to sleep, but she wasn't hungry.

She felt trapped like an animal in a cage and had to get out of her room. She craved the warm night air on her skin as if it would salve her wounds after Zafir's aloofness this afternoon, which had been as good as rejection after her admission that she wanted him. She should never have said those words when they were riding in the desert. She should never have opened her heart, laying bare her emotions and needs for him to discard like yesterday's newspaper.

She wandered out into the peace of the palace garden, now almost in darkness except for the twinkle of small lights along the pathways. The night air was laden with scents from the strange and exotic flowers and above her the sky looked like velvet interspersed with sequins. It was magical and she stood looking up beyond the smooth cream walls of the palace at a night sky unlike any other she'd seen before.

A skitter of warmth ran down her spine and she was sure she could sense Zafir behind her. Did she want him that much? *Yes.* The unbidden answer came.

She could almost feel his touch on her shoulder, his hand lingering there, sending a frisson of heat to every part of her body, and she closed her eyes as his unmistakable scent enveloped her. Was he really here? Had he risked all protocol to come to her? Was this to be their night?

'Destiny.' His deep voice, so sexy, so seductive, proved she wasn't imagining anything.

She didn't dare speak, not wanting to break the spell by turning to him, almost afraid that if her imagination had conjured him up, as soon as she opened her eyes she would be alone. And she didn't want to be alone. She wanted to be with Zafir tonight. She wanted to be his, completely and totally, as the hours of darkness lay over the palace.

Then she felt him against her back, as he wrapped her in his arms, pulling her closer to him, his breath feathering her ear. 'I had to come.' His hoarse whisper broke the soft silence that enveloped them. 'I shouldn't want you, I can't want you, but I do.'

He kissed her neck and she leant her head back against him, allowing him more access. A shiver of anticipation darted around her body as his lips touched every bit of naked skin on her neck.

'Neither of us should want this, but we do.' Her words were a ragged whisper as her heart thudded in her chest. She wanted to turn to him, to press her lips against his, but at the same time couldn't break the tenuous contact they now shared. 'Let's just forget the rest of the world for a few hours, forget everything except what we feel now.'

His kisses stilled and she felt his chest expanding against her back with every deep breath he took. Had she said too much—again?

'I want to forget it all,' he said and pressed his lips into her hair, inhaling deeply as if taking in her scent. 'I want you in a way I've never wanted a woman before, but I can't be like other men. I have a duty to my country.'

'Just for these hours of darkness,' she whispered and opened her eyes to look once again at the stars. 'That's all we need, Zafir, just the one night.'

It was all she knew she could have and the fact that he asked nothing of her only made it easier for her. He expected nothing and therefore there wouldn't be any demands on her. She was safe, in control.

Her eyes widened as she heard the growled oath slip from him. Even though she didn't understand it, excitement raced through her as suddenly he spun her round to face him, his hands holding her arms firmly. She wanted this in a way she'd never wanted anything before and right now she was sure she was the one in control, not only of her emotions but him.

'You are like a witch. You've cast a spell on me and I'm powerless to resist you.'

'Then don't.'

Zafir's eyes were heavy and black with unconcealed passion. His face was as stern as it had ever been, as if he was wrestling with his conscience. Destiny felt desirable. No man had ever made her body ache so badly with need, so wantonly. Somewhere in the back of her mind a warning rang out but she wasn't in the mood to listen to anything other than the singing of her body as he looked at her. She didn't want to heed anything other than the pulse of desire coming from deep within her. She wanted to be his, she wanted tonight—regardless of what tomorrow would bring.

She reached up to stroke the hard angles of his jaw, desire coursing through her as her fingers touched that so perfect stubble. She wanted to give herself to him. A man who freely admitted he couldn't give her what she wanted. A man who represented everything she was trying to escape, one who sought complete and utter control.

With the speed of a falcon swooping on its prey, Zafir's lips claimed hers in a hard demanding kiss. His tongue plunged into her mouth, demanding and erotic. She couldn't believe the flirtatious groan she made, a sound like no other she'd heard before, but she wanted this—wanted him.

In answer his hand splayed on her back, pressing her into him, and she felt the hard ridge of his erection as her hips moved against his, forcing the flames of desire higher still. Her hands wound around his neck, determined that this time he wouldn't go, wouldn't leave her with that unquenched throb of need humming in her body. Her fingers delved into his thick hair, relishing its silky strength.

'This is too much...' His voice broke with huskiness before he kissed her once more, his hand sliding up her body, cupping the fullness of her breast as his tongue once again took up a frenzied dance with hers.

It was mind-blowing and she could hardly stand as the pleasure of his touch made her knees weak. She gasped into his mouth as his thumb caressed her tightened nipple, the silk of her *abaya* and the lace of her bra hardly any barrier at all. But still it wasn't enough, still she wanted more. So much more.

She forced herself to push away from him, finding it hard to catch her breath or even hear herself think above the pounding of her heart. Emotions and sensations she'd never known, never dared to hope to experience were in full control of her now. The inexperienced woman who'd left England was gone.

With a shy smile she slipped her hand into his and led the way to her suite of rooms. His fingers tightened around hers as he followed, giving her all the encouragement she needed.

Walking into the dimly lit room was startling after the near darkness of the garden and she felt him hesitate, draw back and stay on the threshold. He looked into her face, his expression questioning. Was he regretting coming to her?

'What is it?'

'This is all I can give, this night.' The warning there was clear, but so too was the sexy huskiness, giving her the confidence to be someone so different from the woman she'd always been. The last thing she wanted him to think was that she was an inexperienced lover and she definitely didn't want him to know she was a virgin.

'I know,' she said softly, meeting his gaze and tilting her chin up, emboldened by the desire in his eyes. 'I know.'

CHAPTER SIX

ZAFIR LOOKED AT her lovely face and felt as if an arrow had lodged in his chest. Destiny had turned his world upside down, making him take a long hard look at himself, at his life, but still it hadn't changed anything. He wanted her, wanted to be able to change everything so he could be with her for more than just a few snatched hours. But it could never be. Not when duty remained the most important thing in his life, the one thing he could not ignore.

Whatever happened between them, he was still the ruler of Kezoban, a ruler without a wife or heir because of his reluctance to commit. After Tabinah's death, that sense of duty was stronger than ever. He'd forced his sister into an arranged marriage and now he would do the same, but only after being with Destiny. Tonight would be theirs.

'It was by chance that our worlds collided, that we met in England—a chance that has given us this night.' He had to be sure she knew there could never be a repeat of this night and that nobody must know. 'Tomorrow…'

'I know, Zafir,' she whispered and moved closer to him, her eyes darkening to the colour of strong coffee.

'I know you have a new life to move on to, that nobody in the palace can know.'

'It is for your sake as much as mine.' He kept his voice firm, even as desire stirred ever higher. Did she have any idea how beguiling she looked, how seductive? But there was something else; despite the boldness of her actions, an underlying innocence shone through and he wondered just how practised at seduction she was.

She pressed her fingertip to his lips, jolting him with the intensity of that touch, chasing away such thoughts. 'Please don't say any more.'

He kissed her finger gently, then turned and closed the door to the garden before taking her hand and leading her across the vast expanse of marble that was her living room and through to the luxury of the bedroom.

He could smell her seductive scent, light and floral, making him think of England in the summertime, but also reminding him who she was and that making love to a woman in his palace was something he'd never done before. Did that mean she was different? He squashed that thought and focused his attention on the present, the moment he'd tried to avoid but had longed for so strongly for the last two weeks. Making Destiny his—for one night at least.

Destiny's gaze met his and she saw his doubt, his uncertainty briefly before the smouldering darkness of passion filled his eyes once more.

She wasn't sure who had moved, but suddenly she was in his arms, exactly where she wanted to be. She slid her hands down his back, loving the feel of his firm body as his lips kissed down her throat. His hands cradled her breasts, now achingly firm and sensitive as she arched herself towards him.

Anticipation sizzled between them as his mouth covered hers, teasing and light at first, then hot and demanding. She kissed him back, matching his hunger and deepening the kiss until she thought she would pass out.

He lifted his head up, taking his kiss out of reach, and she found herself looking at the dark skin of his throat, noticing the dusting of hairs. She'd been so consumed by need for him, she hadn't realised he was dressed casually in beige trousers and a white shirt made of the finest silk, embroidered with gold as befitting his status.

She smiled at the thought of seeing the man beneath his robes, as he was now and as she really wanted to see him. Had his chosen outfit been a way of coming to her as Zafir the man and not Zafir the Sheikh, the ruler of Kezoban? Right now she didn't care, didn't want to question. He was here and tonight she would be his.

'Something amuses you?' he questioned, his voice deep and regal as he held her away from him, watching her face intently.

'I was wondering if removing your robes would be as easy as what you're wearing now.' She stifled a nervous laugh, realising she'd never teased a man like this before, her experience of intimacy having been less than limited, more like non-existent. Unwilling to allow a man close, she'd given all her devotion to horses. Zafir was the only man who had breached the barrier she'd purposefully erected, made her want more, made her want to experience all the pleasure of making love—even if it was for just one night.

Her gaze slid down his body. Imagining him in his robes, she was aware that if tonight was all they had she'd never find out how to remove them. She pushed that thought to the back of her mind. Just being here, beneath his appreciative gaze, was so far removed from anything she'd done before. The heat of the desert must have changed her, made her a more wanton and passionate woman, one she'd had no idea she could be.

'It is as well that I can discard your *abaya* with ease,' he said and brushed a kiss on her lips, tasting them and sending heat racing through her body.

She tried not to think of how many times he might have done just that, tried to push aside all thoughts of the women who'd been in his life, desperately wanting to stay in the moment, to savour every touch, every sensation of being desired by him.

Instead she pressed her body against his, wanting more than just kisses. She felt again the burning hardness of his body, and heat unfurled deep within her. With a soft sigh, she gave herself up to instincts she'd never known she possessed, moving her hips against him.

Swiftly he pushed against her, giving her no choice but to move backwards towards the bed. His breathing was deep and ragged, echoing her own, as the back of her legs met the bed and she dropped back onto its softness.

Zafir covered her body with his as he took her mouth in a hard and wild kiss. She could feel the fierce intensity of his passion, his lips bruising hers, but she wanted more. Despite the clothing they still wore, she was in no doubt how much he wanted her and with each passing second she thought she might go up in flames.

She wanted him. It felt wrong yet so right. The only thing that was as clear as a star-filled night was that she needed him so very much. She wanted him to be the first man she made love to.

Her nails dug into his back as he kissed down her throat and she arched beneath him. His hand slid down her side, resting on her hip.

'Zafir...' She gasped his name as his tongue caressed her nipple through the silk of her *abaya*. It felt so good. 'I want you, Zafir.'

She reached down between their bodies, wanting to touch him. She fumbled with the fastening on his trousers, revelling in the guttural growl that escaped his lips as she touched him through the fabric, feeling the heat of him. She'd never undressed a man before, let alone touched one like this, but the fire in her veins emboldened her. She was acting on instinct that had lain dormant within her, waiting for him. Finally the fastening gave way and she felt the silk of his underwear, now barely able to conceal him.

He moved suddenly back away from her, bracing himself over her on the bed before lying beside her. All the while his gaze remained fixed firmly on hers, sending shivers of anticipation hurtling all over her. Her heart thumped a little harder when he pulled a foil packet from his pocket and she was shocked it was a consideration she hadn't given even a moment's thought to.

'Before we go any further...' His voice had become a deep husky growl which sent pleasure skittering down her spine and she watched in awe and even a little trepidation as he swiftly rolled on the condom.

His dark eyes held hers prisoner as his hand slid her

abaya up her thighs and he hooked his fingers into her lace panties. She shivered in anticipation and lifted herself up from the bed, enabling him to tug them down. His eyes were laden with desire as he smiled. It was a small smile that barely lifted the corners of his beautiful mouth, but one which sent molten heat coursing through her as he tossed the panties to the floor.

With his dark eyes fixed to hers he moved back between her legs, urgency in every movement, so much so that only the barriers of underwear had been removed. She panicked. Would he be disappointed? Would he know how little experience she'd had? She moved her hips up towards him, surrendering herself to the needs of her body. She felt him touch her, nudging insistently, before thrusting deep inside her.

She gasped as he filled her, and closed her eyes against the sudden pain. She couldn't stop another gasp from escaping, one mostly of satisfaction at having him inside her, of being possessed by him. Momentarily he paused and she felt his whole body shake as he looked down at her.

'Please, Zafir,' she said and wondered if that throaty sound had actually come from her, but already her desire was taking over as she lifted her hips, encouraging him.

In answer to her body's plea he moved within her, setting up a fast rhythm which threatened to sweep her far away. It felt so good, so right.

She clung to him, moving her hips faster and deepening every thrust into her he made. It was exquisite. She felt as if she were on the edge of a cliff, barely able to balance. She wanted to fall, wanted to give in to the pleasure of it, yet wanted to enjoy the moment of being with him for just a few seconds longer.

His arms shook as he balanced himself above her and she slid her hands inside his shirt, moving them across his back, desperate to feel his skin. Each move he made took her closer to the edge until she knew she had no choice. She couldn't hold on any longer. She had to go over. Her head fell back as she gasped in pleasure at the sensations rushing through her. He cried out, thrusting hard and deep into her, sending her over the edge until she no longer cared where she was, just as long as she was with Zafir.

Slowly her body floated down to earth, leaving the stars behind, and she opened her eyes, aware of the weight of Zafir's body on hers. His heart was pounding, echoed by hers, and his breathing was still fast and hard. It had been wonderful, more beautiful than she'd ever dreamt, but his words of warning came rushing back to her.

This is all I can give, this night.

'I'm sorry.' Zafir's voice was low and full of concern. 'It should not have been like that for you. I should have had more control, more thought for you.'

He stood up from the bed and disappeared into the bathroom. Her heart plummeted. How should it have been? What should she have done? Should she have told him she'd never had sex before?

She sat up, dragged her *abaya* down and clasped her knees to her chest. She closed her eyes against the rush of emotions engulfing her as she heard water running in the bathroom.

Was her night of passion over already? Well, if it was, she wasn't going to let him know how much it hurt.

* * *

Zafir stopped when he came back into the bedroom and watched as Destiny curled her knees up and dropped her face onto them. It was such an innocent movement, reinforcing what he now knew for sure. That despite her flirtatious teasing, her provocative words of desire, she was inexperienced and innocent.

She'd been a virgin and he'd taken her in a heaving rush, with scant regard for her pleasure. So intense had his need been he hadn't even removed his clothes. He hadn't seduced her as he'd planned, hadn't explored her glorious body while he lay naked next to her—he'd been nothing more than an eager youth demanding his own satisfaction.

He'd wanted to take things slowly, to seduce her and enjoy every moment of their short time together, but she'd been his undoing. Her kisses had inflamed a passion deep within him like no other he'd ever felt before. All sense of control had slipped away into the dark desert night.

He sat on the bed next to her and she looked up at him. Her brown eyes were wide and watchful. The forced smile on her lips twisted his heart and he touched her face softly. 'I'm sorry. I should have been gentler.'

'Why?' Her voice croaked with raw emotion and he ached to hold her, to ease the pain he'd caused. 'Because I'm inexperienced and it was my first time?'

Her stark words lanced through him but he couldn't look deeper into what they meant to him; he didn't want to acknowledge the tradition that as a ruler, a man of power, he should never take a woman's virginity, unless it was that of his wife. He pushed those thoughts away. Right now he had to make things right with Destiny.

He shook his head as he slid his palm across her cheek before pushing his fingers into her hair, holding her head, preventing her from looking away. 'Because you deserved more than that. I was like a teenager, eager, crass and totally selfish.'

She smiled at him, a real smile that reached her eyes, making them sparkle. 'No, not you.' She laughed softly, a sexy sound that made his pulse race all over again. 'You could never be that, not when you are the Sheikh.'

'And because I am the Sheikh, you should have told me you were a virgin,' he said, forcing his tone to remain soft as the guilt finally hit him.

'It's not exactly something a girl wants to admit, especially to a man like you. But isn't that why you came here tonight as the man I met in England, not the man who rules Kezoban? I expect nothing from you, Zafir. You made that very clear. We have only one night.'

He felt something tighten in his chest, as if he was being squeezed, and he knew she was right. He had come to her as Zafir, the man, in an attempt to shake off the guilt which just having her here in the palace was intensifying. Out of duty to his kingdom he'd forced Tabinah into a marriage she didn't want and yet in complete disregard for his duty he wanted to go to Destiny, a guest in his palace and a totally unsuitable woman.

Despite the war between duty and desire raging within him, he couldn't leave her yet. He might have behaved like a sex-starved youth, taking her so quickly, but now he wanted to hold her, to feel every part of her against his body and give her the pleasure and satisfaction she deserved. He wanted her more than ever and the hours of darkness were still around them. This was still their night. Tomorrow would come soon enough.

Slowly he leant towards her and brushed his lips over hers, whispering against their softness, 'Can you forgive me?'

Her hand caressed his cheek before she kissed him. It was a soft lingering kiss which set fire to his blood all over again. No woman had ever made him feel so hot. Never had he lost control like that so spectacularly. Yes, it had been a long time since he'd sought the pleasure of a woman's body, but that was no excuse for such animalistic behaviour.

'Only if you take me to bed,' she said shyly and looked into his eyes.

'I promised you a night of pleasure—' just thinking about her naked body made his voice turn hoarse '—and there are many hours before dawn in which I intend to make amends.'

'Promises, promises,' she teased, her fine brows rising suggestively, her innocent eyes darkening with desire.

'This time,' he said, standing up, taking her hands and pulling her up to stand before him, 'we'll take it slowly.'

The air around them sparked with sexual tension as he began to remove the silks from her body. She moved with him, lifting her arms until everything was just a crumpled heap on the floor. He watched as she slid her hands behind her back, undid her bra and dropped it to the floor, leaving her completely naked.

'You're so beautiful,' he said, not wanting to touch her yet, wanting to gaze at her pale skin, glowing in the lamplight. His gaze moved down to her breasts, watching them move slightly with each breath she took, her nipples dark, hard and so tempting.

Slowly he undid his shirt, enjoying the hungry look in her eyes as she watched him. He dropped his shirt on top of her discarded *abaya* and feasted his eyes on the thick curls nestled in the apex of her thighs, feeling himself harden with desire.

'And the rest,' she said, stepping closer to him, her light floral scent weaving around him once more.

He pulled the remaining foil packets from his pocket, tossed them onto the bed and removed the rest of his clothes, leaving only his underwear. She quirked her brows suggestively and he pulled the silk down over his hips and moved towards her, taking her naked body against his.

He kissed her, delving his tongue deeply into her mouth, entwining with hers, as his hands moved over her silky skin. She was so beautiful. Tonight she was his and if he discarded his duty and guilt it felt completely right, as if they were meant for one another.

Destiny savoured the warmth of his bronzed skin against hers. Her breasts were so sensitive that the coarse hair of his chest against her nipples almost sent her over the edge again. She smoothed her hands down his back, over his buttocks, pressing him closer against her.

'Zafir,' she gasped as his lips left hers. She felt as if she was the one about to lose control as thoughts of pushing him back onto the bed and sitting astride him ran riot in her head. She'd never done anything like this before, had no idea how to take the lead. But with him it was different, as if her body knew his and knew exactly what to do.

Swiftly he swept her off her feet, cradling her against him as he walked over to the bed. She pressed her cheek against the firmness of his chest and inhaled his virile musky scent. In that moment her whole body burned with need and she bit her lip as he placed her on the bed.

Naked and aroused, he stood before her. She drank him in, from the wide shoulders to his firm chest muscles and the dark chest hair which arrowed down over his flat stomach. With hands that shook slightly she reached out and touched him, the heat of him arousing her further. He groaned in pleasure as she wrapped her fingers around him, exploring and pleasuring him.

Suddenly his hand grasped hers and he swore in his native tongue, his voice rasping. 'You're pushing me too far,' he growled as he lowered his body down next to her. 'When I go I'm taking you with me and I'm not ready to go there yet, my little desert minx.'

Destiny arched her back as his fingers slid down over her stomach and into her curls, teasing her until she squirmed against his hand. Then, slowly, his fingers slid inside her and she bucked against him, closing her eyes, trying to hold on to herself.

'Let go,' he whispered as he leant over her, his tongue twirling around her nipple.

'Zafir…' she gasped as his fingers went deeper and his teeth nipped at her. 'It's too much.'

'Let go, Destiny,' he said against her breast, his breath warm on her moist skin.

Suddenly everything splintered around her and her body floated away on the tide of passion, drifting endlessly on sensations she'd never felt before. She could feel him kissing down over her stomach, but was powerless to move as the ebb of desire carried her away.

Slowly she came back to reality and opened her eyes and looked directly into Zafir's handsome smiling face. She pulled him to her, wanting his lips on hers once more. His body covered hers as he kissed her with fevered passion, then suddenly he moved, pulling her with him until she sat astride him.

A blush crept over her cheeks. Had he known that was what she'd wanted to do?

She leant down and kissed him tenderly, her hair falling forward, creating a dark curtain around them. His hands moved over her back and down to her bottom, bringing her intimately close to him, and he moved upwards to her, sliding deep inside. She moved with him until reality hit her like a flash of lightning across the night sky.

'Zafir,' she gasped as she felt him insistently moving within her, as if he was on the brink of losing control, of claiming her as his once more. 'Protection—we need protection.'

'See what you do to me,' he rasped out as he withdrew and reached for the condoms he'd carelessly tossed on the rumpled bed earlier.

She smiled down at him, kissing him once more, this time eagerly welcoming him into her. It was like nothing else she'd ever experienced and throwing back her head she cried out as he took her over that edge once more, his own ragged groan letting her know he was with her.

For some time after she lay on him, feeling the thud of his heartbeat slow and inhaling his smell, knowing it would be burnt into her memory for ever. Trying not to think of what tomorrow meant, she moved off him until her body was curled against his. His fingers traced a slow pattern over her naked back, becoming lighter as sleep claimed him.

A tinge of sadness formed around them as she lay against his sleeping body. She was painfully aware of the hours ticking by. This was all she ever would have of him. He'd warned her, but still her silly heart wished for more. What woman wouldn't with the man she'd fallen in love with?

Zafir stirred, moving against her naked body, pulling her close against him. He mumbled something in his native tongue. She didn't have a hope of knowing what he meant, so kissed him gently, smiling when, through the haze of sleep, he responded.

In the dim light before dawn she could see his eyes were heavy with sleepy desire and the simmering heat inside her bloomed once more. His lips were soft and coaxing, the urgency of earlier now forgotten in a moment which seemed more loving than passionate.

Slowly and more gently than she'd ever imagined possible, she became his once more, knowing that the first tendrils of dawn would soon be slipping across the sky and this would be the last time she would ever be his.

For the first night in a year Zafir had slept without the intrusion of nightmares of Tabinah. He knew why. The reason smiled shyly at him as he opened his eyes. 'Good morning, beautiful,' he said softly and brushed his lips over hers.

Why couldn't every morning be like this? Why couldn't every night be like last night?

He felt his body tense as the answer hit him as if he'd woken to one of England's cold and frosty mornings. Nights and mornings could never be like this because he was the ruler of his kingdom and a man who *had* to put duty before his own needs.

'I really don't want to—' he moved to prop himself on his arm and look down on her; with dark hair spread across the pillow and passion-dazed eyes looking at him, he had to steel his body against the urge to make love to her one last time '—but it's time I left. I am already late for my morning ride and wish to avoid any speculation.'

'I know.' She smiled up at him and his chest constricted, making breathing difficult for a moment. 'We had one night. Now we must return to our own worlds.'

He blinked in shock, not having expected her to be so brutally honest. It dented his male pride to think she didn't want to cling. Already he knew it would make his need for her stronger, more intense, but he couldn't waver. He had to move forward in his life, do his duty, not just for his kingdom but the memory of Tabinah. It was time to select a bride from those who'd been chosen for him.

'Yes, Destiny, we must.'

He thought of the meetings planned for later that month, meetings that would procure him a bride— the woman with whom he would produce heirs for his country.

He clenched his jaw.

Duty again.

Always duty.

Duty had destroyed his relationship with Tabi-nah, forcing her to take such drastic actions. Those actions and his guilt now dictated that duty was his only choice.

CHAPTER SEVEN

LATER THAT DAY Destiny found concentrating on her work harder than ever, especially when Zafir arrived to watch her working with Majeed. She could barely function, just thinking of him and the hours they'd shared last night. Each image which came to her mind made her heart flutter and her pulse race. It certainly had been a night she would never forget, but it was over and time to move back to a professional relationship.

One quick glance at Zafir as he stood watching her, arms folded, his expression almost fierce, confirmed that. He would be expecting nothing but detached professionalism from her and that was what he'd get.

One night was all he'd been able to give. One night was all she'd wanted. One night to imagine what being loved would be like, but she hadn't anticipated it would be this hard the next day. She'd thought she was freeing herself, allowing herself to sample the pleasures of being with a man like Zafir without the complications of love, which for her mother had been the start of all her trouble.

Focus, she told herself as dust from Majeed's hooves in the sand rose around her. She was here to do a job. What had happened last night was not and never would be part of that arrangement. But, try as she might, she couldn't keep her mind from wandering and she certainly couldn't continue working with Majeed. Not with Zafir's brooding presence so close. She'd told him once she preferred to work without an audience, but perhaps it was time he was reminded of that, put herself back in control.

As if sensing her distraction, Majeed came to a halt and looked at her, his eyes watchful and his ears alert. She had at least gained the stallion's trust, but she knew that gaining Zafir's trust would never be possible. For whatever reason, he shut himself away and even last night, in the depth of passion as they first made love, he had guarded his soul. In the hours that followed, before dawn had lightened the room, she'd seen the real man and what being loved by Zafir could be like. It made her long for more, but she knew it was a futile dream.

'That's enough for today,' she said to Majeed and the stallion walked towards her and waited until she began to lead him back to his stable.

'You have made remarkable progress with him.' Zafir's words warmed her and not just because he was pleased, but because he was close—much too close.

She should have expected Zafir to join her. Of course he would want to know just how well his horse was responding to the hours she was spending each day with him. What she hadn't expected was the way her body heated, the way her skin tingled and the way her stomach somersaulted as he walked beside her or the way she yearned to have him close.

Thank goodness the stable boy was around to take Majeed from her. She was in grave danger of turning to Zafir in the hope he'd take her into his arms and kiss her as he had done last night. She knew they couldn't have any more so why was she grieving for something she'd never really had?

'I am confident that he will go beyond the palace walls before I leave.' Home was the last thing she wanted to think of. The idea of returning to England and leaving behind the man she'd given her virginity to was too much. How could she possibly turn her back on what they had?

But what did they have? He'd made it clear it was for one night only, that there could be no more than that.

'Walk with me back to the palace.' He didn't look at her and the superior tilt of his chin warned her it was far from a request. Unexpected anger zipped through her. He expected her to do just as he wanted, proving he was as controlling as her father. But didn't he have a right to be? He was her boss, even if temporarily, *and* he was a Sheikh, a ruler. Didn't that give him every right to want to be in control?

'We do not have an escort,' she pointed out, challenging him and his superiority.

He watched as the stable boy led Majeed away, then he turned to her, his eyes dark and his brows heavy. She couldn't help but look at his full lips and remember the kiss that had set fire to her so spectacularly. She could still feel the roughness of his trimmed beard on her skin.

'I don't give a damn. After last night things have changed.' The intensity in his voice shocked her.

'Nothing has changed, Zafir. I will return to England in a month and you will select your bride. Last night changed nothing. You made that very clear and I accepted it.' How could she be so bold, standing her ground so strongly when her whole body hungered for just one last caress, one final kiss?

He took her arm and led her casually away from the stables, but from the rigid line of his back she knew he was feeling far from casual. As they entered the cool arched walkways that ran the length of the palace, he stopped, forcing her to do the same. She turned to look up at him, noting the firm set of his jaw.

'Do you really expect me to forget last night so easily?' His voice deepened, the sensual tones sending an exotic shiver all over her.

'It is what you wanted.' She kept her words firm, not wanting him to know just how much she really wished he couldn't forget last night.

'Things have changed.'

'What things?'

'You gave me a precious gift and after such a gift I do not intend to turn my back on you yet.'

Destiny's mind fumbled for answers. What was he talking about? 'A gift?'

He stepped closer to her and she had to fight the urge to close her eyes against his scent. 'You gave me your virginity, Destiny. Have you any idea how potent that is? Or what it means to me?'

'I don't understand.' Was he saying he still wanted her, that what they'd shared was special?

'You are now mine.' His voice had softened, becoming so sensually seductive it was impossible to do anything other than look up at him, into the unfathomable darkness of his eyes. Her heart raced. Zafir didn't want to turn his back on her or the passion they'd shared, but his next fierce words shattered that illusion. 'I will come to your suite tonight.'

So it was all about possession—his possession of her.

Before she could say anything else, Zafir's aide came briskly towards them and she wondered how long he'd been near and if he'd seen them or, worse still, heard Zafir's words.

The thought of Zafir returning to her suite this evening sent ripples of excitement through her, despite his obvious domination. The tingles of excitement intensified as he looked across at her, the first sparks of desire in his eyes, and she could barely walk calmly beside the two men as they made their way along the maze of corridors.

Once again, Zafir stopped abruptly as they neared the guest suites. His aide thankfully walked ahead and then paused, but the suspicious frown on his face didn't disappear when Zafir moved close enough to her to whisper quietly, 'I will send your maid.'

'Mina? Why?'

'Doesn't every woman enjoy being pampered? Especially when she is expecting her lover.' His dark brows snapped together, but the polite cough of his aide prevented anything further and Destiny was left to watch him turn and stride away in a flurry of white cloth.

Was that what she now was? His lover?

Very soon, Zafir's intentions became clear when Mina all but forced her into a deep scented bath and began what Zafir had referred to as pampering. Did he ensure all his women were treated this way? Was she now one of his women? His latest mistress?

Zafir made his way through the palace gardens as night fell. All afternoon he'd thought of nothing else but Destiny, her soft pale skin, her silky hair and brown eyes which always held a hint of shyness. She was there in his mind with everything he did and had been since he'd first seen her that day at her home. Last night had only intensified that.

He thought again of the moment he'd realised she was a virgin. Had she any idea of the implications of allowing him to be the man who took that from her? She should have told him. It was something he'd needed to know, something he'd had no right to take. Deep down he was profoundly glad she hadn't said anything because, if she had, his conscience would never have allowed him to make love to her and he would never have known such completeness as he'd experienced last night. It had been so intense, as if they were destined to have come together.

His body hummed with anticipation as he entered the small private garden of her suite. He expected to find a contented and pampered Destiny waiting for his arrival, but she sat curled on the cushions in the living area of her suite, a cold and distant expression on her beautiful face as she looked up at him.

'Would you mind telling me what this is all about?' She held out her arms to show off the silk of her outfit, the kind worn by women all over his country, giving them modesty, but on Destiny it fuelled his ardour, making him want nothing more than to remove the bright coloured silk. The short tone of her words was the only thing holding him back from taking her in his arms and continuing what they had started last night.

'You did not enjoy the pampering?' He was so stunned he couldn't move and strangely found himself not in control of either his emotions or the situation.

'Any woman would enjoy all that has been lavished

on me this afternoon—if they were a woman of your harem.' The last words were spat at him, reminding him of the feral cats that roamed the old city's streets, hissing and spitting if anyone got too close.

Despite his earlier reassurances, she truly believed he had a harem—and that she was now one of his women! The idea was so absurd he laughed, which only irritated her further. With fury burning in her eyes she stood up, looking almost as lovely as she had when passion and desire had replaced her usual shyness last night.

'I do not have a harem. That is not my way. I am a man of honour and have been faithful to any woman I have had a relationship with, as I will to my future wife from the moment our marriage is announced.' A sliver of guilt sliced through him. He had honoured the rules his father had instilled in him as a teenager. He'd kept his affairs brief and far away from the palace—until last night. Honour was something he believed in as strongly as duty. Nothing would ever change that, not even a beautiful Western woman who'd sent spirals of turmoil through his life from the moment he'd first set eyes on her.

'So why this?' Again she held her arms wide, the silk of the gown she wore clinging to her curves in a way he'd never noticed on other women.

'I thought only of your comfort. You work hard. Hot dusty work. I thought you'd appreciate feeling more feminine.'

'Well, I certainly feel more feminine now.' She walked across the room away from him and sat at the farthest point she could, but he would not be deterred. His body still hungered for her, still wanted her, and he knew she was far from indifferent to him. Just as he had when he'd led the life of a single man, he was enjoying the chase, the challenge.

He poured a cool drink, passing her one, then purposefully walked towards her before taking a seat opposite her. He took a sip of the cool lemonade he'd learnt she was partial to and then placed his glass on a nearby table.

'That pleases me.' He held her gaze as a spark of attraction fizzed around them. 'And now I'd like to talk.'

'Talk?'

He might want to take her to bed and make her his once more, but after last night he needed to know more about her life, her reasons for making such a hard deal with him. Somehow she'd ensnared his interest, his passion and all he wanted was to know more—much more.

Her defensive attitude warned him he needed to use caution—that she could bolt as easily as an unbroken horse. He had no idea why, but he couldn't let her go now. Not yet.

'Yes, talk. Do you have an objection to that?'

'No.' She looked doubtful but her voice was much less defensive. 'What do you want to talk about?'

He knew he should address the concerns his aide had tentatively raised only hours after his aide had seen him leaving her room. He'd been warned she would be expecting more than he could give. The direct and unusually outspoken but trusted aide's voice was grating on his nerves. Were the palace walls so alive that his night with this woman had become common knowledge?

The thought angered him as much as the marriage

he must make for the good of his country. He was not ready for that commitment yet, but had no choice. He needed an heir.

Destiny's mind whirled. Zafir had sent Mina to pamper her until the whole suite was fragranced with new and exotic smells. She'd dressed her in gorgeous new silks and, although the maid had said nothing, Destiny was sure she'd known it was her ruler's intention to visit her at nightfall. He might not have a harem, but it appeared that spending the night in a woman's suite was accepted and maybe expected.

Now she sat alone, far from relaxed, and trying to put aside the hurt that he thought he could make her little better than his mistress while she'd given him her heart. Not that she'd ever let him know that.

The only sounds in the suite were those of the desert at night but, inside her head, her heart was thumping as she waited. Anger at his assumption she would go along with his demands and excitement at seeing him again, of having him to herself for a few short hours, mixed together in a swirl of confusion, making her light-headed. When he'd silently walked in from the inky blackness of the palace gardens he'd looked even more magnificent than he had last night. This time he wore his robes, their whiteness stark against the darkness behind him, and she had to fight the urge to go to him, to accept anything he was offering because this time he was Zafir, the Sheikh of Kezoban, a man to be obeyed.

'We need to talk, Zafir,' she said as firmly as she could manage, but the husky undertone to her voice didn't sound very convincing and she resisted the urge to add that she wanted to clarify that he expected nothing more of her because she didn't want to expose herself to the pain of love. She couldn't allow herself to feel anything for him and would have to guard her heart against it because she didn't want to be like her mother.

'Yes, we do.' He stood before her, as regal and handsome as he looked standing in his office as the ruler of Kezoban. 'I would like to know more about you, more of your time in England.'

His dark eyes never left her face and, even though distance separated them, she could feel him close to her. Her body was warm and content after last night, wanting more of those wonderful hours spent in his arms. She wanted to be his once more.

'Is this some sort of test to see if I am suitable mistress material for the supreme Sheikh of Kezoban?' She couldn't alter her defensive attitude. It was her wall of protection. Behind that wall she was safe, able to control whatever it was that had leapt to life between them last night as soon as his lips had touched hers, as if he'd branded her his.

'There is only one woman who can be suitable, as you know. The woman I select to be my wife, the mother of my heirs.' His tone had changed to icy-cold and she knew she was playing a dangerous game, but she needed to play it, needed to cruelly prove to herself there wasn't any future in wanting a man such as Zafir Al Asmari, Sheikh of Kezoban.

'So what are you doing here?' Her heart broke a little as the implications of his words sliced through her. She'd lost her virginity to him, given him her heart, yet she would never be anything else to him other than just another woman. She would never be suitable.

'It is my belief that our paths were destined to cross, as your name suggests. You were meant to be here, meant to heal Majeed. I see now that you have healed me, enabled me to move on to the next chapter of my life.' The firmness of his words left her in no doubt that he actually believed everything he'd just said, but what about the things he hadn't said? Did he believe it was his right to take her heart and break it, while she healed his?

Anger simmered dangerously close to the surface.

'And what is that next chapter? Your marriage?' Why did she feel so disillusioned? She'd known long before his scorching kiss that he was about to take a wife, that he needed a son. Even as she'd given herself to him, she'd known there would be nothing beyond that night. He'd made that perfectly clear and she'd thought she was in control. His presence here again tonight proved how wrong she'd been. He had been in control all along.

He stood and came towards her. Her heart fluttered at a ridiculous rate, making her light-headed.

'I want to know why.' He sat next to her, the exotic spices of his scent opening up memories of their night together, making images of their bodies entwined on the white sheets of her bed spring to mind.

'Why what?'

'You were a virgin, Destiny. Why me? Why last night?' He leant towards her, his dark eyes heavy with desire. Was he recalling their first night together as vividly as she was?

'I wanted to give myself to a man who wouldn't ask for more, a man who couldn't have any control over my feelings.' Heat rushed over her, colouring her cheeks and she lowered her lashes. How could he ask her that so boldly, so calmly, as if he had a right to know everything about her?

'What did you hope to gain, coming to Kezoban?'

'Gain?' Shock raced through her. He thought she'd slept with him for gain? Fury quickly doused all other emotions. 'I have only one thing to gain from being here in your country.'

'And that is?' His heavy brows rose, arching in total superiority. What had she been thinking, giving herself to this man, falling for him like a teenager? He was nothing if not in total control of everyone and everything. He was worse than her father.

'My freedom.'

Now it was his turn to be shocked and she enjoyed the moment of satisfaction that she'd been able to knock the wind from him. But it was short-lived. As ever, he was quickly back in control, quickly able to hide his emotions behind a stern and commanding expression.

'Explain.' The order was all but snarled at her.

He'd baited her long enough, see-sawing her emotions from extreme highs to lows at his whim and now she was angry.

'My father is exactly like you.'

He laughed, a bitter sound, his contempt clear. 'That is not possible.'

'Oh, but it is. He is cold, hard and equally as driven as you, but the trait you have in common is the need to control people, to dominate.' The tirade wouldn't stop and all her hurt from the past collided with her confusion about this man, making an explosive cocktail. 'I only agreed to be here so that, like my sister, I could escape his and my stepmother's rule. I need to finally begin my life now that I no longer have to look out for Milly.'

'Explain.' Again that one word snapped out in a furious command.

'My mother married my father when she realised she was expecting me. It was a marriage that would not have happened otherwise. She loved him but he did not love her. I wish I could have asked her more about it, but sadly she died giving birth to my sister. As Milly and I grew up, my father became harder and more controlling. I have helped Milly to set herself up in London and now I intend to do the same.'

'And that is why you drove such a hard bargain before agreeing to come to Kezoban?'

'Precisely. When I thought I was dealing with your aide—if you remember?'

'Then it is wealth you crave?'

'Why else would I be here? Why else would I have tried to seduce you?'

If he thought she was only sitting here with him, dressed like a woman from a sultan's harem, to get as much as possible financially from him, then so much the better. He wouldn't want to whisper tantalising sweet nothings as they made love and her heart would be safe. It would make creating distance between them so much easier.

'If it is only money you want, then I have a new deal to put to you.'

'What kind of deal?' Her head spun. He'd turned the tables yet again to his advantage. Once more he was in control.

'In less than three weeks I have to announce my marriage. Arranged marriages are not made for anything other than material gain. Therefore, I want to enjoy my remaining weeks as an unmarried man—with you.'

What was he trying to say? 'You mean you want to buy me? Pay me to be your mistress until you take a wife?'

Shock raced around her like lightning across a black sky. How could that one passion-filled night have come to this? He'd made it very clear that they would only have one night and now he was dangling more, much more, before her, tempting her, but would it be enough? Instinctively, she knew she had to be as cold and calculating as he was. She had to demand more from him, be the woman he obviously thought she was.

'I want only to make a deal that will give us both what we want.' He snapped the words out, his impatience as clear as a star-filled night.

'Very well. Double our original deal.' She kept her voice hard and her face set firmly as she looked at him, wishing with all her heart he was asking her to stay because he wanted her. How could she still want him, still hunger for anything he could give? Her childhood had taught her there was only one way to deal with such a man—to stay behind her protective barrier and be equally as cold.

Irritation and anger infused Zafir as Destiny made her demands, just as she'd done the day he'd first seen her. At least this time he knew her motives. His aide had been right, but that still didn't lessen the sexual chemistry which sizzled between them.

For the first time ever he didn't care about anything else. He wanted her—at whatever cost, emotional or financial, he didn't care. He had to spend every available minute with her before he entered into a contracted marriage, one that duty to his kingdom and guilt for the loss of his sister demanded he made.

'It doesn't have to be so businesslike,' he said softly and moved towards her, wanting to abandon himself once more to the ecstasy he'd found last night. Now she'd named her price and they'd struck a deal, he wanted to bring things back to how they'd been last night, when they had been nothing more than lovers coming together. A brief and passionate interlude in time.

She didn't move away from him and the parting of her lips told him all he needed to know. Despite her rigid posture as she sat among the cushions, she was as drawn to him as he was her. As compelled by desire as she had been last night. She was still his.

'But we have just made a deal. Doesn't that mean it is business?' Her voice was a whisper. Only hints of her earlier bravado lingered.

'We have just discussed the terms of our deal, yes, terms that will give us both what we want.' He stroked the back of his finger down the softness of her cheek, the quickly drawn in breath telling him all he needed to know. 'Now forget it. We need to explore the fire between us until it dwindles to cool embers.'

'What *is* between us, Zafir?' The earnestly asked question halted him and he looked into those soft brown eyes, now swirling with desire. How could he answer that when he didn't know himself? Damn it, he didn't even want anything to be between them. She could not be his destiny, his future, despite her name.

'Something that shouldn't be there, but is.' He

looked at her lips, so soft and inviting, wanting nothing more than to feel them beneath his. Whatever it was that had exploded to life between them that one night was now calling to him again. He was like a man possessed. All he wanted was her. 'And I cannot walk away from it—not yet, not until every last flame has been extinguished.'

'One night,' she whispered as her pupils enlarged, obliterating the soft brown of her eyes almost completely. 'That was all you said we could have. Just one night. So why more?'

'I have a duty to perform, Destiny. I must select a bride from a list chosen for me. Duty is the mantra by which I have lived my life and marriage is a duty I cannot avoid, but I am not yet married and, for a short while, I want to give us a chance to explore the attraction which exists between us. Can you deny it is there now, drawing us closer, despite everything?'

'But...'

He silenced her protest, pressing his lips to hers, kissing her like a man who'd been in the desert for many days. As he pulled her close, he relished the feel of her body against his and knew he didn't care about anything other than making her his once more. For two weeks he was free to be a different man, one not bound by duty and obligation to his kingdom.

For two weeks she would be his.

CHAPTER EIGHT

FOR TWO WEEKS Destiny had lost herself in the oblivion of being with Zafir and she had to force herself to remember it was nothing more than lust, that she was in Kezoban only to secure her future and her freedom from her father. It would be so easy to fall in love with Zafir and it was only the knowledge that she was just his latest mistress that kept her from doing so.

There had been times she'd wanted to call and confide in her sister, but the mere fact that she was having such a relationship with a man like Zafir would set the alarm bells ringing for Milly and she didn't want to worry her when they were so far apart. Neither did she want to admit that those alarm bells were also sounding in her own head.

Zafir represented everything she'd always wanted to avoid in a man. He was controlling, dominating and so handsome women would surely fall at his feet. And she'd done the same, as if drawn by forces she had no understanding of and little ability to resist.

As days had turned to weeks, she'd known he would announce it was over, that it was time for him to do his duty and select his bride. But how could she go back to her life in England and forget the passion, the desire they'd shared each and every night?

The first light of dawn crept in, tracing intricate patterns on the marble floor as it shone through the carvings around the archway and, as always, it signalled Zafir's return to his suite, to his duty as the Sheikh of Kezoban. But, just as last night had felt different, this morning was different too.

Instinctively, she knew exactly what was happening—their time together had come to an end. His insatiable need for her last night had been about goodbye, but she wished he'd warned her. Instead now she would have to pack up all the memories of being with Zafir and stand back whilst he chose his bride.

'I am leaving the palace today.' He turned onto his side, propping himself on his elbow and looked at her, but she couldn't meet his gaze, not when her mind was so full of wishful thinking. 'I shall be away for at least a week.'

She forced herself to be as strong as he was and sat up in bed, looking at him, but she didn't trust herself to say anything, not yet, not when her emotions were so dazed by something she'd known all along would happen.

Zafir sat up, pulling her close, kissing her with a passion which lingered from the night and she couldn't help herself. She moved closer against his naked body, the sheets of the bed only just allowing her some modesty.

'And when you return, you will be engaged.' It wasn't a question but a statement. She'd known all along that she could never be more than a passing affair for him, his final mistress before he married, but it still hurt, still cut deep.

He sighed as he moved, swinging his legs to sit on the edge of the bed, giving her a tantalising view of his strong bronzed back. She wanted to reach out and stroke her fingers over his skin, to feel his strength and power in every muscle, but he was no longer hers, even though she would always be his.

'It is my duty.' He stood up and, unashamedly naked, crossed the white marble floor to the robes he'd discarded last night with such haste. She drank him in, committing every last bit of him to memory. He pulled the white robes over his body and his dark gaze met hers across the expanse of her bedroom, the fire of passion now extinguished. Already he'd distanced himself. 'I am expected to produce heirs for my country.'

'I know,' she said firmly, determined not to cling to him or what they'd shared. She would show nothing but dignity and strength. 'My work with Majeed is almost complete and I will soon return to my life in England.'

She forced herself to think professionally, although her state of undress made that difficult, and clutched the sheet against her. She had to remember why she was here, why she'd even agreed to Zafir's demand that she work with his horse. She was in danger of falling in love with a man who could never love her, just as her mother had done. Replicating more of her mother's life story was her biggest fear.

The ever-present shadow of how her mother had died haunted her, making motherhood an almost impossible choice. So even if Zafir told her right now he wanted to make her his wife, she couldn't, not when children would be of paramount importance. She just couldn't risk leaving her child alone in the world, not when she and Milly knew only too well what it was like to lose their mother so young.

'You will come to my office before I leave—to discuss Majeed's progress.' The briskness of his tone told her he'd already switched from lover to Sheikh. What they'd shared was over.

'As you wish.' There was a crisp edge to her voice too, one born out of the need to survive. 'Once I have finished working Majeed, I will come directly to your office.'

He stopped and looked at her, his eyes as black as midnight, glittering in a way she'd never seen before. His heavy brows snapped together and she instinctively clutched the sheet tighter against her. This was not the way she'd envisaged their affair ending, not with such harshness on his handsome face.

He didn't say anything but held her gaze for a moment longer before striding out of the room and towards the doors which led to the palace gardens, as usual avoiding being seen by anyone in the palace. She knew he would now ride in the desert, then attend his duties before flying his hawk, a routine he'd kept to for the last two weeks. Had that been as cover for their secret nights together?

Pain rushed through her. Why had she allowed herself to become not only his mistress, but his secret mistress? A guilty pleasure he could never acknowledge. She'd barely even kissed a man before she'd arrived in Kezoban. So what had changed so drastically?

She was late. Zafir paced his office, waiting for Destiny to report on Majeed's progress, still irritated by her cool acceptance of his intended departure and now her inability to keep her word. He seriously considered marching down to the stables to see her. Had she been so pliant over the ending of their affair because she thought she had new power over him?

That would be a serious error of judgement. Nobody had power over him. He was the only son of the Sheikh of Kezoban—he'd been taught to be commanding even from a young age. Anything less would have been to let his father down, a man he'd admired and wanted to please. When his father had died he'd become the youngest ruler Kezoban had ever had at just twenty-four and now, six years later, the days of doing what he wanted were over. He had a duty to his people, his country—even Tabinah had failed to understand that.

He growled an oath, causing his aide to look suspiciously at him. For the first time in his life he wished he didn't have a duty to honour to his country. He wished he could be free to be the man Destiny wanted. The man she needed. He'd had affairs before, broken the ties many times, but never had it been as hard as this morning. As she'd looked at him, defiance shining in her eyes, he'd forced himself to remember that duty *had* to come first, which meant his feelings towards Destiny must be sacrificed. He'd made his father a promise just before he'd died, to always put his duty to Kezoban before anything and it was one promise he intended to keep.

As if conjured up by his thoughts, a servant entered, escorting Destiny to his office. This would be the last time he saw her before duty consumed him, taking him along the path of an arranged marriage. He had no real wish for marriage, but after Tabinah's death it was necessary, not only for the succession of his family as rulers of Kezoban, but for the promise he'd made to his father.

As Destiny walked in, he noticed her chin was just a little higher than usual and a spark of defiance glittered in those lovely eyes. Was this as hard for her as it was for him? Did she yearn for more nights like those they'd shared? He pushed the thought savagely aside. That was all in the past and it was time to do his duty and move forward.

'How is Majeed?' He kept the subject on the reason for her presence here in his kingdom, in his life. The reason she'd driven such a hard bargain. If he asked how she was, he would want more. He would want to hold her, to kiss her and make her his again, but he'd done that in the early hours for the last time and it couldn't happen again.

'His progress is good. He is responding well now and my work will very soon be complete.' She looked straight at him, her eyes hard, almost brittle. Beside him, he knew his aide was watching them. He could feel the other man's questions and suspicion, sense the scrutiny that was barely concealed. Anger simmered inside him. If it was so noticeable that there was something between him and Destiny then all his care to protect not only her reputation but his had been to no avail.

He'd never before so much as touched a woman in his palace. The life of a bachelor prince had been played out on foreign shores. The fact that Destiny had tempted him to even consider such an affair, right here in his palace, spoke volumes for the intensity of the attraction he had for her. But he could not act on it any longer.

Zafir turned on his aide, the harshness of his voice

122 THE SHEIKH'S LAST MISTRESS

unintended. 'Leave us,' he commanded in English so
that Destiny would know what had been said.

'Sire?' the man questioned as he looked at him.

'Leave us.' The command in his voice reverberated
around the white walls of his office and for a moment
he thought he saw Destiny flinch, but when he looked
at her properly she was as defiant as he'd ever seen
her—and beautiful.

'I thought discretion was needed.' Her words
slammed into him as the door of his office closed
with a loud click behind his aide. 'If that little display
doesn't alert suspicion it will be a miracle.'

'I am the Sheikh and I am about to leave the palace
to meet with the families of potential brides. I insist on
just a few moments alone with you.' The words fired
out as he gave vent to his irritation.

Her gorgeous brown eyes, so full of emotion,
sparked with fury as she glared back at him. Her lips
were parted and he remembered how she'd kissed him
as passion had engulfed her. She was beautiful, tantalising and almost everything he needed in a woman—
but it could never be. He would be a fool to consider
continuing with such a union. How could he when he'd
forced Tabinah into an arranged marriage, making her
so unhappy she'd fled the palace under the cover of
darkness?

'We've had every night for the last two weeks,
Zafir. Each and every one of them was more than "one
night." It's time to move on with our own paths in
life—different paths which should never have crossed.'

She stood firm and rigid. Was she so immune to
him, so closed to the pain of saying goodbye that she
could stand there like a regal princess who'd been

trained since childhood to be so aloof? Such natural poise and decorum proved she could be a suitable bride.

Where had that thought come from? He'd never considered Destiny as anything other than a lover, even though she'd been a virgin. They were of different worlds, different cultures and beliefs, brought together only by their common interest in horses.

Zafir looked at her again, as if seeing her with new eyes. Sunlight streamed in around her from the archways and beyond her lay the desert and, dressed as she was, in clothing of his country, she looked as if she belonged, as if she'd been created especially for the role. Especially for him.

But being his wife was a role. The woman he married would need to be strong of mind and wilful in spirit. She would need to be someone the women of his country could look up to but at the same time she had to be prepared to be one of them. More importantly, she would need to provide him with healthy male heirs to continue his family's rule and enable him to fulfil the promise he'd made to his dying father.

Fury boiled up. How could he consider marriage for his own selfish reasons when he'd denied Tabinah exactly that?

'You shouldn't have dismissed him.' Destiny's sharp words snapped him back from the brink of thoughts of what could never be. When he looked at her everything in her stance seemed to confirm not only that she could be all the things he needed but that she was, as if fate was pulling them ever closer.

'You are right.' He turned and marched to the ornate arched window which looked out over the desert, the vastness as empty as his life now seemed, knowing Destiny would no longer be in it. But she was right. She had a life in England and he had duty to his family name, his country.

He refocused his thoughts. 'I should not have sent him away. It was remiss of me.'

As he turned to face her once more, he thought he saw disappointment on her face. He watched as she swallowed, and remembered kissing her neck, tasting the pale creamy skin as she'd lain beneath him, totally consumed by desire.

He shouldn't be having such thoughts. Passion and desire had never played a serious part in his life. Never had he been able to live far from the shadow cast by the role he'd been born into and yet, somehow, something was changing, shifting like the desert sands, making him long for something different, challenging the duty and honour which drove him.

'I will leave before you return from your trip.' The tone of her voice gave nothing away and he fought hard against the urge to go to her, to pull her into his arms and make her come back to life, make her want to be his again. This Destiny was cold. Too cold.

'As you wish.' He stood behind the gilt-trimmed desk, hoping to gain some strength from its solidness. He'd never been this emotionally weakened before, but then he'd never had two weeks of passion-filled nights with a woman who set every nerve on fire and stirred needs and desires he'd constantly pushed aside. 'I will make the arrangements. Mina will inform you when it is done.'

Destiny opened her eyes and, just as had happened for the last two mornings since Zafir had left, a heavy weight of despair settled over her, pressing her into the bed. It was still early and she tried to close her eyes and sleep, but the hurt caused by Zafir's lack of emotion or any hint of compassion as they'd talked in his office made her feel physically sick.

She turned restlessly in the bed to face the windows, watching as the daylight chased the darkness away, remembering Zafir leaving her bed, often reluctantly, to slip quietly through the gardens and back to his suite before resuming his usual routine.

That man had been a different man to the Sheikh she'd last faced, the one who was now able to switch off his emotions, making her doubt he'd ever had them. It hurt to acknowledge the last two weeks had all been about sex for him, his final act of recklessness before he settled down to do his duty—marriage for the good of his country.

It should have been as unimportant for her too. It was how she'd wanted it to be. She turned in bed again, trying to push back what she felt, deny its existence, but she couldn't.

She'd done the worst thing possible. She'd fallen in love with Zafir.

She closed her eyes against the pain of knowing he'd never love her and tried to ignore the nausea which claimed her, churning her stomach so severely she wanted to cry. She never cried. She was strong—she'd had to be and she always would be—but now she was so low, so heartbroken she couldn't even face dressing and going to the stables.

For the first time since she'd arrived in Kezoban there wasn't the smallest amount of pleasure or excitement in spending several hours working with such a magnificent stallion as Majeed. With a groan she buried her head beneath the pillow and begged for the oblivion of sleep.

When she woke again it was late and Mina had arrived with a breakfast tray. It was a treat she usually relished, but this morning, knowing she'd said goodbye to the man she'd given her heart to, breakfast, no matter how enticing, was the last thing she wanted.

Her stomach lurched and, without her usual greeting to Mina, she slipped quickly from the bed, dashing to the bathroom, where she splashed cold water on her face in an attempt to quell the heaviness which sat like lead inside her. She looked at the pale reflection of herself and closed her eyes against the washed-out image. How had she come to this? How had a man penetrated all her barriers and attacked her heart? She'd never wanted to be so vulnerable, always telling herself she would never love a man who didn't show her love. Yet she'd done just that when she'd fallen for Zafir.

Finally she returned to her room to find Mina had set out her breakfast on the table beside the open doors which led to the terrace and the gardens, but the idea of sitting and eating was the last thing she wanted to do. In fact just the thought brought the earlier nausea back with a vengeance.

'I have made a new tea for you,' Mina said in her accented and gentle voice, making her sound very motherly, which provoked a new urge to succumb to tears. 'It will help to put some colour back into your pale face.'

Destiny was too emotionally out of sorts to argue or be aggrieved at the comment and sat looking out at the garden and the path which wound its way through the exotic plants towards Zafir's private garden—the path he'd walked many times as he'd secretly visited her to spend the night in her bed. Nights that would never happen again.

Destiny took a sip of the warm tea, more to please Mina than to satisfy any need of her own for food or drink. The tea was fresh and reviving and settled the heartbroken queasiness of her stomach. Was this what it was like to be lovesick?

'This is good.' She smiled at Mina, who looked pleased. 'I guess I'm feeling a little homesick.'

'You do not like my country?' The older woman's smile had dropped and a worried frown creased her brow. Destiny realised she would miss Mina's kindness when she left.

'I love Kezoban. I'm really happy here, but my work with Majeed is almost over and it's time to think about going home. In fact can you arrange for me to leave earlier than planned?'

Once the words were said and she'd committed herself to leaving Kezoban, Destiny's sense of equilibrium returned. Today she would ride Majeed out of the palace. He was ready and had been for some time. She'd just put it off in order to stay in the dreamlike state she and Zafir had lived in for two weeks. But all that was over. Zafir had had enough of being the playboy Sheikh meeting his mistress in secret and wanted to return to being the duty-bound man his country believed him to be.

She had what she wanted—distance from her father's control—and, thanks to the deal she'd struck with Zafir, a means to start her new life in a flat near Milly. Thoughts of her sister crowded in on her and, not for the first time, she wished she could talk to her, but there would be time enough for that when she re-turned to England. Right now she had one more hurdle to cross with Majeed, then her job would be completed. She would be free to go, but she knew she'd never be entirely free of this desert land or its ruler. He would always be in her heart.

She dressed in her usual clothes for working with Majeed and Mina watched as she returned from the bedroom, an uncustomary look of concern on the older woman's face. She liked Mina, who was like the mother figure she'd lost when her mother had died so suddenly. Tears prickled at the back of her eyes as she thought of not having Mina around and inwardly she cursed the unfamiliar highly emotional state she'd slipped into.

She really must sort herself out. It was time to re-gain control of her life once more. Time to move on and admit her newly realised love was a lost cause. Zafir had made it clear when he'd bartered for more time with her that it could never be permanent or pub-lic. She only had herself to blame and now it was time to put it all behind her. She would finish her work with Majeed and leave.

Several hours later, she realised she'd had no idea of the time—she'd been so pleased with Majeed's prog-ress, his trust in her—until the nausea had combined with tiredness and heat, forcing her to seek shade. She knew she shouldn't have stayed out so long. The sun scorched down on her and, despite the scarf which cov-ered her hair, she felt as if she was on fire.

The shade of the large rocks at the foot of the moun-tains she'd ridden past with Zafir the morning of their ride would offer some respite from the heat and a chance for both her and Majeed to rest.

The stallion stood silently after she'd slipped to the ground to sit on a rock. She tried to push from her mind the story of Zafir's sister being bitten by a venomous snake, taking comfort in the fact that Majeed was calm, which meant he at least didn't sense any danger.

'Just a little while and then we will head back,' she said as much to herself as the horse. Suddenly Majeed's head lifted, his ears pricked forward. 'What is it?'

Destiny hoped it was someone and not something that the horse had heard, but when he whinnied she almost jumped and forced her weary limbs to move as she stood, gathering up the reins and trying to ignore the way her head spun. 'We'd better go.'

With more effort than she'd ever needed, she mounted Majeed and, as she pushed him out from the shade of the large rocks, he whinnied again. She glanced quickly around, anxiously scanning the ground for slithering forms, but the pounding of approaching hooves made her look up and out towards the desert sands.

Zafir.

What was he doing here?

Like a fantasy image, he was riding fast towards her, the long grey mane of the stallion flying out and his robes joining in the speed-induced dance. A cloud of dust billowed behind him and all she could think about was that he'd come for her, that he couldn't stay away, that wanted to be with her.

As he drew closer, Majeed shifted restlessly but that didn't alarm her nearly as much as the anger she saw etched in Zafir's face, anger which didn't fit with the thoughts she'd just been having. Once again she'd got it all wrong.

He pulled his grey stallion to a halt, dust spiralling from the ground, and Majeed spun round, anticipating some excitement after standing quietly in the shade with her. She tried to keep her gaze focused on Zafir but the effort made her dizzier than she cared to admit.

'What are you doing here?' she snapped at him, trying hard to control the thud of her heart at the image he created. He looked wild and untamed and the thud of desire leapt to life within her. As Majeed continued to prance excitedly her stomach lurched uncomfortably.

'I could ask the same of you. Have you taken leave of your senses?' His raised voice was hard, killing any last hope of him wanting her.

'I was doing my job. The one you contracted me for. To take Majeed out beyond the palace walls.' Majeed shifted restlessly beneath her and she forced every ounce of strength she had into her words. She would not be dominated by this powerful Sheikh. The attitude which radiated from him now was exactly what she wanted to escape.

'Come,' he demanded and turned the grey stallion around.

Before she had a chance to answer, he'd pushed the horse into a gallop, dust flying upwards in its wake, and Majeed reared up, waiting for her command to follow. Only the slightest pressure of her legs was enough to propel him forward and after his master. Majeed's fast pace jolted her, doing little for her unsettled stomach, and it took great effort to stay on board. Finally the palace was in sight and Destiny breathed a sigh of relief. Her head was spinning and her stomach lurched uncomfortably as the pace slowed to a trot and then

thankfully a walk. All she wanted was to rest, to close
her eyes and block everything out.

Zafir's blood fizzed in his veins as he marched ahead of
Destiny, back towards her suite, sensing her following
with every muscle in his body, but he was too angry
to heed that now. What the hell had she been thinking to take Majeed out into the desert alone—in the
heat of the day? The anger that had rushed over him
as he'd learnt she'd brought forward her departure date
had intensified as he'd ridden hard across the desert,
knowing instinctively she'd be in the very place he'd
taken her that morning they'd gone out, the same area
that Tabinah had lost her life.

Guilt thrashed at him again and he gripped his
hands into tight fists as he entered the suite, to find
Mina waiting anxiously, the relief on her face at seeing Destiny behind him short-lived when she realised
just how angry he was.

'You will rest.' He turned abruptly to Destiny, causing her to almost walk into him. The urge to reach out
and steady her was intense, but he couldn't. Not yet.
His emotions were running wild and he had to analyse them first, get himself completely back in control.

How had she managed to creep beneath every barrier he'd ever erected around his heart? How had she
been able to make him feel, make him care for her?
Worse still, how had that care changed to something
much deeper, something he just wasn't able to accept,
let alone act on?

'I have packing to do.' Her flippant reply tested him
further, but the paleness of her face worried him and

he recalled Mina saying she'd been unwell for the last two mornings.

He tempered his reply. 'First you rest, then you can prepare to leave. My plane will be at your disposal whenever you should choose to leave Kezoban.'

'My work is done now, Zafir. I want to leave— tomorrow.' He noticed the slightest rise of Mina's brow at Destiny's familiarity in addressing him, but he didn't care any more what anyone thought. Right at this moment he wanted Destiny to stay for a little while longer at least and give him the chance to deal with the way she made him feel. The fact that he now wanted to put her above his duty to his kingdom, even above the guilt he felt over Tabinah's accident, was alien to him. He couldn't think past it yet.

'I understand that, but I wish to hold a feast for you. A mark of my appreciation.'

'That is not necessary.' She walked across the room and pulled her scarf from her head, letting her hair tumble free, again heightening Mina's speculation as to what was going on between them. 'You have paid me to do the work.'

'It is tradition,' he impatiently tossed at her, wishing they were alone. But then perhaps it was for the best they were not. 'You may leave after the feast.'

Without waiting for her response he strode from the suite, marvelling at how a woman he found so attractive could be so infuriating. He was not used to his decisions being challenged—and she'd challenged every single one from the moment they'd met.

She'd also challenged his duty, the memory of his sister and the promise he'd made to his father.

CHAPTER NINE

THE NEXT MORNING, as the pink rays of dawn spread across her bedroom, Destiny felt the nausea return and she knew. She couldn't dress it up as homesickness any more. She had to face the truth. She was pregnant with Zafir's baby. Acknowledging that, even silently to herself, made everything not just terrifying but much more complicated.

Could it really be possible when Zafir had always been so careful? *Almost always.* There had been just that one time during their first night together when they'd been so consumed with need for each other that she'd had to remind him of the need for contraception. Was it possible that brief moment had been enough?

Fear speared through her as the nausea engulfed her, but it wasn't fear of facing Zafir—it was fear of being pregnant. What if she became ill like her mother? If only she'd had those tests done—tests that would re-assure her she wouldn't have to leave her baby alone in the world. A baby that wouldn't have an older sister to care for it, bring it up and protect it from the wrath of a dominating and controlling father.

She pressed her hands against her eyes, fighting nausea and fear as they battled for supremacy. If she had this baby she could die, but that wasn't what she feared most—it was the thought of leaving behind a baby.

So far she'd made every mistake her mother had made, from falling in love with a man who wanted nothing but to be in control to getting pregnant with his child. There was only one part of the pattern left to replicate.

Zafir certainly wouldn't want to discover she carried his child, not when he was about to make a marriage, one that would provide heirs for his kingdom. Legitimate heirs. She closed her eyes against the thought of how he would react to such news. She needed to see her doctor, the one who knew her mother's medical history. She dreaded what she might be advised to do about the pregnancy, but still there was no way she could tell Zafir yet.

All she needed to focus on was leaving Kezoban as soon as possible, but definitely before Zafir sought her out this afternoon.

As the room lightened she packed her few belongings and then took her mother's diary, holding the tattered box with suspicion. Had keeping such a thing, bringing it with her, been a bad omen, meaning she'd do exactly as her mother had done? She inhaled deeply against a fresh wave of nausea, then stuffed the box hard into her bag, trying not to think too much now.

She couldn't cope with such questions; she just needed to get home. But where was home? Her father would be furious about the deal she'd made with Zafir, but even more so when he discovered that she was returning pregnant—a fact she couldn't hide for

long. There was only one place she could go and that
was to Milly's.

With haste she dressed in her usual clothes, forgo-
ing anything but the headscarf for modesty. She didn't
want to arouse anyone's suspicion, especially Mina's.
It would hurt to leave the friendly face she'd come to
rely on without saying goodbye, but it was for the best.
As far as she knew, the plane she'd asked for would be
ready to take her away from the desert kingdom and
the ruler she'd foolishly fallen in love with.

She put the final belongings into her bag and zipped
it up. Mina could arrive at any time with breakfast. Just
the thought of that made her even more nauseous than
she could cope with, but she forced herself on, needing to be ready to leave as soon as possible.

She pulled her headscarf tighter, then picked up
her bag and took one last look at her room, especially
the bed where she'd discovered the joys of loving, the
bed in which she'd given everything to Zafir and conceived his child. Thoughts of him brought tears to her
eyes but she shut them tight. Crying was something
she hardly ever succumbed to and now she knew why
it was all she'd wanted to do lately, but tears were for
later, not now.

With a sigh she turned and made her way to the
door, only to see it open and Mina walk in carrying a
breakfast tray, followed by a younger maid, carrying
the most gorgeous deep purple and gold silk *abaya*.
Mina directed the other maid to leave the *abaya* before retreating. As the door closed behind her, Mina
frowned, glancing down at the bag she carried as she
crossed the room to place the tray on the table by the

open doors as usual. 'The Sheikh has requested your presence in his office as soon as you have eaten.'

The efficient tone of the maid gave nothing away but, even so, she would be sorry to leave her. 'Thank you. I will go there now—before I leave.'

'You are leaving? Now? What of the feast tomorrow? The Sheikh has sent a gift for you to wear.'

Destiny looked at Mina, not sure if the older woman would sympathise with her if she knew all the facts. What was she doing, thinking she could confide in a member of Zafir's staff? Pregnancy was really muddling her mind. Gift or no gift, she had to leave.

'Yes, now.'

'Are you well enough?' Mina's dark eyes met hers, unsettling and questioning. Destiny had the distinct impression that Mina knew she was pregnant with the Sheikh's baby. She thought back to the ginger tea she'd first prepared several days ago. Was it possible that Mina had known long before Destiny herself had acknowledged the sickness for what it was?

Dread raced through her. If Mina knew, had she told Zafir? Her loyalties would certainly be with her ruler. 'Of course I'm well enough. I just need to go home now my work with Majeed is done.'

Mina stepped towards her and took the bag from her, which she let go of without a fight. 'Eat some breakfast, then see the Sheikh before you make any more decisions.'

'There is nothing more to stay for,' she said quickly, panic at the thought that Mina might have informed Zafir making her legs weak and her head spin. She didn't want to inflict on herself, or her baby, a life empty of love because, although she loved Zafir, she knew he didn't and never could love her. Even if everything went right and she could go ahead with the pregnancy, she had no wish to raise her child in the shadows while he raised a family with his new wife.

Her mother's diary told the same story. It left her in no doubt that her mother had hoped for so much more when she'd become pregnant with her first child. She'd wanted love and the kind of happy-ever-after Destiny seriously doubted existed. Those longings had poured onto every page and she'd read the page which told her why she'd been named Destiny many times since.

Her mother had believed a baby would bring her closer to the man she loved, but her father was the same kind of controlling man as Zafir. He was as hungry for power and the unexpected birth of a child had not been what he'd wanted, but he'd done his duty and married her mother.

The horror of her mother's death, the blood disease she herself could have inherited, rushed at her. What if she had complications with the birth? What would happen to the baby if she too became a victim of that disease, as her mother had? It was why she'd been adamant she never wanted marriage or children.

'But there is time for breakfast,' Mina urged gently, so that those stupid tears threatened again and for a brief moment Destiny was tempted to confide in her. No. If Zafir didn't already know he most certainly would then. He had to be free to do what his position in life dictated. She didn't want to stop him doing what he needed to do, not when she might never be able to have the baby, a thought which was as devastating as the fear of following in her mother's footsteps.

The idea of putting off this last encounter with Zafir

suddenly became far more appealing. If she lingered at breakfast, maybe he would be busy with other work and unable to meet her. Much to Mina's delight, she sat at the table and tried to look delighted with the array of sweet pastries and fruit before her, but her stomach turned and it was almost impossible.

'I have made the ginger tea again—to help with the sickness.' Mina's words confirmed her suspicions. Of course the woman would know the signs of pregnancy. She'd probably served many women.

Destiny nodded. 'Thank you.' She couldn't say anything else. All she could do now was go and see Zafir and hope that he didn't know, then she could leave, allowing him to make his marriage deal. Only when she'd seen her family doctor could she decide how and when she would tell him.

Zafir stood by the desk as Destiny entered. She looked pale but a determined strength shone from her eyes. Had he got it all wrong? He was sure Mina's near insolence as he'd demanded to know where Destiny had taken Majeed had been an attempt to highlight not only Destiny's health but the reason for her current pallor.

He'd played that conversation over and over in his mind, convinced that it had a deeper relevance. It had been Mina's very insistent mention of sickness over recent mornings which had set alarm bells ringing.

'She is not well, sire.' He could still hear the worry in her voice as the words whirled in his head.

'Not well?' He'd swung round to face the maid, wanting an explanation.

'For the last two mornings, sire, she has been unwell.' Mina's usual subservience had been absent and she'd looked at him earnestly, but all he'd been able to think of was Destiny out on Majeed in the heat of the day, when she wasn't well. He hadn't wanted to hear anything else and had marched from the suite, but now he wished he'd demanded a full explanation instead of accepting hints that Destiny was suffering from morning sickness.

Just as when he'd galloped across the desert to find her, he knew that if Destiny had become pregnant from their union it would change everything. The child she carried was his child, his heir, and he had a duty towards that child greater than the duty to make an arranged marriage. In all probability, the child had been conceived the night he'd taken her innocence, which in itself tied him irrevocably to her.

He wanted to ask Destiny but, for a man who always guarded his emotions, he was overwhelmed with this unexpected news. He knew he wouldn't be able to put it into words without giving away his excitement at the prospect of being a father and what this turn of events meant for them—that his duty was now to her and their child...that they could be together.

He wanted to pull her to him, kiss her and tell her he'd do his duty, he'd look after her and the baby, but still she hadn't said anything and the underlying suspicion that he'd misinterpreted Mina's words, or that she herself was mistaken, was still a real possibility. He would have to allow Destiny time to break the news herself.

As soon as she did he knew exactly what he'd do. It wouldn't be the duty he'd always envisaged, of making an arranged marriage and producing heirs, but the duty to his unborn child. The duty of not a ruler, but a father.

Much to his annoyance, Destiny didn't say anything and he noticed for the first time her Western clothes and the obvious attempt to distance herself from him.

'You will not be able to leave today. A goodbye feast is organised for tomorrow and the next day my plane will be available to take you back to England.' He hoped she wouldn't need that plane but he saw panic in her eyes as she turned to him.

She was beautiful but distant. In her brown eyes was the same spark of suspicion and discontent he'd often seen in Tabinah's eyes during the months after her marriage had been announced. She had resented everything he'd done for her, all his attempts to make her life as comfortable as possible. He'd failed her, driven her to flee on the back of a horse she wasn't able to handle. He'd pushed her to it and he would feel guilty for that for ever. Had he pushed Destiny away too?

'A feast isn't necessary. I would rather leave today—now.'

'That will not be possible. It is tradition here in Kezoban to hold such a feast for a visitor. It will be done and you will attend. I have sent a new *abaya* for you to wear.' He couldn't tell her how significant that *abaya* was, that the colours were his and that by wearing it everyone would know even before he announced their marriage that he was claiming her as his wife.

'I need to leave now, Zafir. Today.'

'And offend my people? Offend me?'

Her eyes widened in surprise but otherwise she remained as calm and unruffled as a bird of paradise.

Would she really be so calm if she wanted to tell him she was expecting a baby? His baby. His heir. Yet still he trusted Mina's instincts.

'Can you assure me I will be free to leave after the feast?' The demand in her voice was clear and he wondered how he was ever going to turn the conversation towards her *illness*.

He walked towards her and she stood tall and firm. It was as if she wasn't carrying such a powerful secret, one that would change their lives beyond recognition. Overnight his duty had changed, become conflicted with all that he'd grown up knowing he had to do. He had as much duty to his child as he did to his country—if not more.

'You will be free to leave the day after the feast—if that is what you want.' He hesitated, strangely out of his depth, a sensation so new it unnerved him.

'It's what has to be done.' She looked at him, a fire in her eyes so completely opposite to the desire he'd seen smouldering within them that he couldn't help but step towards her.

'You're right,' he goaded. 'We both have our lives to lead, lives that should never have crossed, and now that you have completed your work with Majeed we must return to those lives.'

'Precisely,' she said and stepped away from him. 'Now I will leave you to your work.'

She hadn't said a thing about being unwell, hadn't hinted at anything to suggest she might be carrying his child. He couldn't let her leave Kezoban without knowing for sure. Anger rushed through him and he took a deep breath. He was not used to having information withheld from him, but letting his emotions rule, displaying how he felt, would not help the situation. Calm control was required.

'Destiny.'

She whirled round and looked at him. 'Yes?' Briefly he thought he heard a hint of hope in her voice. The small tremor in that one word pushed him on, that and the fact that he had to know. But he also had to hear it from her. She had to want to tell him. He had to exercise patience, the valuable lesson he'd learnt from the tragedy of losing Tabinah. That dreadful time had taught him that at least.

'Is there anything else?'

'No. Should there be?' Destiny's stomach turned over. The dark and brooding look in his eyes screamed suspicion. Did he know? Had Mina told him the secret she herself had only just discovered? She was more convinced than ever that the maid knew about the nights she'd spent with the Sheikh.

'I believe that there is.' He moved towards her and she stepped back as he came close, but breathed a sigh of relief when he walked past her to the large double doors of his office. That relief was short-lived when he turned the key in the lock.

Expectancy hung in the air as he looked at her. 'Are you going to tell me why you have been ill these past few days?'

'Heat, I guess.' The words slipped from her lips but she couldn't look up at him, couldn't look directly into the eyes of the man she loved and lie.

It's just until you are married, until you've kept your promise of duty to your father—and until I know if I can even have this baby.

She hated doing it, but she couldn't be the one who stood in the way of his duty. Her mother had paid the price of forcing a man into marriage because of pregnancy; it had all been written in her flowing handwriting. There was no way she was going to force Zafir into any kind of commitment.

He moved closer to her, his height towering over her, and she had no choice but to look up at him. She could see the dark stubble on his face, the glint of steel in his eyes and the clench of his jaw. Her head began to swim and the nausea she'd pushed successfully away returned with a vengeance.

Her body became like lead and the sensation of sliding to the floor overpowered everything. Then she felt the strength from Zafir's arms as he caught her, smelt his scent as she was pressed close against his hard chest and she closed her eyes, giving in to the need for oblivion—her need for him.

When Destiny opened her eyes she was in her room, on the softness of her bed, and Zafir, like a guard, was standing over her at the end of the bed. She glanced quickly around to see if Mina was there.

'We are alone.' He snapped the words out and she knew his mood had darkened. Alert to the prevailing sense of danger, she forced her weary limbs to sit up on the bed, the soft pillows behind her offering some comfort.

Still he wore that closed and cold expression and her heart sank. She knew she had to tell him not only that she was carrying his child, but that she would be leaving and would never want anything from him. What she couldn't put into words was her fear and the guilt she felt at not wanting his baby.

That fear was why she'd immersed herself in her love of horses, never looking for marriage and a family. All she'd ever thought of was that last entry in her mother's diary. She was scared that she too might have problems during childbirth which could take her life and leave her baby alone—and she knew what that was like.

'Zafir, what we shared was special, but it can never be. *We* can never be. Our lives are too different.'

He scowled at her, his eyes narrowing in suspicious anger. He reminded her of the hawks she'd seen him fly once when he had no idea she'd been watching. Just another image she would have to block from her mind, cast to the back of her memory.

'Sometimes changes happen and differences are brought closer, blending to become one.' His poetic words were sharp and the tone of his voice hard. If he'd said it softly, full of meaning, she would have had to stop herself from telling him that such a change had occurred. They would always be joined by the new life within her. A life she didn't even know she could give birth to safely because she'd stubbornly refused to be tested, preferring to hide behind the disguise of not wanting to be a mother.

But those poetic words hadn't been said with any trace of emotion, not even the smallest hint of the love she felt for him. She couldn't tell him, not yet. It would be better if he went ahead with the marriage he needed to make and she returned to England, where the payment for her work in Kezoban would enable her to seek the best medical help and, hopefully, reassurance that her fears were not founded in fact but the lasting pain of losing her mother. Only once she knew she could have the baby would she tell him—providing he'd done his duty and married, because she had no wish to repeat the example of her parents.

'I need to go home, Zafir. Back to England.'

'No.' That one word snapped out and she drew in a breath so sharp she almost couldn't breathe. Where had the gentle man who'd showed her the joy of love-making gone? What had happened to the man who'd kissed her so tenderly she'd wanted to cry? Why had this hard, cold and emotionless man replaced the man she'd fallen so deeply in love with?

'I *have* to go.' She leant forward, ignoring the swimming sensation in her head as she did so. The most important thing was to get away, as far away as possible before her heart broke completely.

'That is no longer an option.' He moved from the foot of the bed, his robes sighing softly and all she remembered was his body as she'd explored him for the first time, touching and kissing him. Heat suffused her cheeks when she finally met his icy gaze as he stood looking down at her, his eyes hard and unyielding. She had to push such crazy thoughts from her mind, had to focus on getting away, back to England.

'But,' she stammered trying to think through the fog in her mind, 'I have to go home.'

'You will not leave today.' His voice deepened and, if at all possible, the hardness in it became more pronounced. 'You are not well enough to travel that distance, not unless you see a physician.'

'Then I will rest and leave after the feast as planned. I'm just tired and a little exhausted by the heat.'

Through the hurt of losing the man she loved and the shock of discovering the very real possibility that she was carrying his baby, she conceded his last words were at least right. She wasn't up to going anywhere right now and she did need to see a doctor, but not until she was back in England.

'You will not leave this palace without my knowledge.'

She looked at him, amazed that the icy tone of his voice as he laid down conditions he had no right to make had become almost arctic. How could a man of the desert, a man so passionate, become so cold? She knew that the little colour her earlier thoughts had put in her cheeks was draining away rapidly as shock settled over her like an icy blanket. 'Not leave the palace?'

'You look very pale again. Perhaps I should send for my physician?'

'No,' she blurted out. That was the last thing she wanted. There was no way she wanted anyone knowing she might be carrying Zafir's child. It was bad enough that Mina suspected, but would a maid be in a position to divulge such a secret? She certainly hoped not. 'I'm fine. I will rest and leave tomorrow, as I said.'

'You will not be leaving tomorrow or the day after.' He looked at her, sparks of anger in his eyes, his jaw clenching beneath the finely trimmed beard, and in that moment she knew that her secret was not hers alone any more. He knew. Everything he'd said since she'd opened her eyes made sense now, from the need to rest, to the physician, to the changes that brought differences closer. He knew, but still she challenged him.

'Why not?'

He folded his arms across his broad chest as he

took in a deep breath and a sense of impending doom seemed to breathe from him, enveloping her completely. 'You will not leave Kezoban. Not when you are carrying my child.'

CHAPTER TEN

DESTINY COULDN'T SPEAK, couldn't even think. To hear Zafir say those words aloud sent a chill down her spine. He knew and, what was worse, he knew she'd kept it from him and that she'd had no intention of telling him. How did she now tell him she didn't want his child because she'd never been brave enough to have the blood test, even when Milly had? How did she say she might have inherited the same disease which had claimed her mother's life soon after Milly had been born?

Her past crowded in on her like a dark storm cloud, heightening the fear she'd been running from since she was a teenager and even more now that she was pregnant. Even though her pregnancy hadn't been confirmed, Mina's reaction to her morning sickness meant that clinging to any hope she'd got it wrong, that she wasn't pregnant with Zafir's child, was foolhardy.

'No, Zafir. I can't stay.' Finally she found her voice and it shocked her to hear the hardness within it. Whether it was in response to Zafir's cold detachment, a way of protecting her heart from further pain, or that she was still so numb with shock, she didn't know, but she sounded utterly heartless.

'Do not say that again, Destiny, not when the child

that grows within you is my heir.' The use of her name tricked her into looking into his eyes, their blackness deeper than space and so much colder. An icy chill slipped over her and she shivered, hugging her arms against her as she sat on the bed. Zafir no longer wanted her as he had during those illicit nights together. All he wanted was the child she carried.

'I am not staying. I *have* to go back to England.' She held his gaze, the frigid intensity of his almost turning her to ice. How could he be so cold, so unfeeling after all they'd shared? *Because he doesn't love you.*

He stepped nearer to the bed, closer to her. 'I will not permit it.'

'You can't keep me here, Zafir. I will not be your mistress, hidden away. I need to go home.' She couldn't tell him it was more than that. She was in love with him and she couldn't tell him the terrifying truth that she didn't even know if she could have the baby. If she went home right now and had the test it wouldn't stop the worst results coming back. And then what would she do?

'And you cannot deny me my child.' The harshness of each word as they were thrown at her made her eyes close against the pain of everything. When she opened them again he was still glaring at her, suspicion and mistrust in his eyes.

She swung her legs off the bed in such a sudden movement of determination that it not only made her dizzy, it forced Zafir to step back, taking with him that dominating presence and, thankfully, giving her room to think.

She stood up, trying hard not to grab on to the post at the corner of the bed for support. She couldn't let him know how weak she felt, how scared and confused she was. She didn't want to be commanded and controlled by him—or any man.

There wasn't any choice. No matter how hard it made her sound, she had to tell him. She swallowed down the bitter taste in her mouth and looked up at him.

'I cannot think about having this baby at the moment.' The words sounded strong and firm as they echoed around the room and she had the satisfaction of seeing his heavy brows furrow together.

'Cannot or will not?' The gritty anger in Zafir's voice only made her determination not to be pushed into something she couldn't do even stronger. Whatever he said, she had to go home and take the test. No matter how hard it was going to be.

'What I decide to do is not for you to worry about. You have my word I will be discreet, that this will not affect you in any way.'

'Not affect me?' The cold, barely controlled anger in his voice almost destroyed her confidence.

'You have your duty, your marriage to make and your life to lead.' She turned to walk away. She didn't know where, when his brooding presence filled her suite. If she could just walk away right now, she would. Fear spiked a fizzy kind of confidence into her, the kind she'd never had and she casually tossed her words over her shoulder. 'And I have mine.'

'Don't you dare walk away from me, Destiny.' Command rang in his voice, pushing her that bit further away, making her love for him seem unreal and totally impossible, as if she'd only dreamt it. But if she had truly dreamt about him, he would have loved her too. He would be with her as she faced possibly the worst moment of her life. If he loved her and was there to support her through it as she finally had the tests, could she do it then?

'You are mine and I am not about to let you go yet.' Each word destroyed that little ray of hope. Of course he didn't love her. She was just a possession. Those nights they had spent together had been about possession and now he wanted to rule her and the baby.

Adamant she was doing the right thing, she paid no heed to the warning in his voice, or the vibration of anger, and continued towards the doors which led out onto the terrace, to the very place she'd first thought he would kiss her. That night seemed to belong to another lifetime.

'Destiny.' Her name angrily rang out, frustration in every syllable. She couldn't blame him. She wanted to hide from him and the truth of the situation. She stood looking out over the exotic gardens, kept healthy and green by his innovative hydro schemes, something she couldn't help admire him for. Not that any of that mattered now. His voice rang out, clear and commanding, as he joined her outside. 'You cannot walk away from me.'

She wished with all her heart that she could, but instead turned to face him, every limb in her body rigid with anger. How had she ever thought he'd be different from her father? He was even more controlling and had been from the outset. Hadn't he hidden his identity to get exactly what he wanted?

'You cannot control me, Zafir. I will not be controlled by anyone. Not any more.'

'That is where you are wrong.' He stood immovable, anger coming off him in waves, the rise and fall of his chest hinting at the battle going on inside him. 'You are carrying my child, Destiny.'

She dragged in a deep and heavy breath, desperate to force oxygen into her body, anything that would help her stand upright and face him. She felt so weak she wanted to crumple to the floor but this was a battle that had to be fought right now. She had to get back to England, had to see her family doctor and face up to having the tests done. Whatever came after that she'd face, with Milly's help and support. She didn't want Zafir involved and neither did she want him to do anything out of duty.

'It is your illegitimate child, one that will be nothing but a disgrace to you.' She flung the truth at him, expecting him to recoil from it. He was the Sheikh of Kezoban, the man who ruled the country and openly admitted that duty and honour were the principles by which he lived. He'd hidden their affair, so how could he possibly want to acknowledge his child?

'How can you say that?' He moved quickly towards her until he stood towering over her, reminding her how it felt to be held by him.

Somewhere deep inside her a flare of recognition leapt to life, her body swayed towards his and she couldn't fight the urge to briefly close her eyes. When she opened them and looked up at him, the sparks of anger in his were subdued by desire. Could it be that he too was resisting whatever it was that still hummed dangerously between them? She couldn't deny it. There was still something there, a connection which threatened to combust, dragging them back into its heated core at any moment.

She couldn't give into it. Things had become so much more complicated. He wouldn't want to support her through this when he was about to make a marriage contract that would be so beneficial to his kingdom.

'We were never anything more than a passing affair.' She tried to make her words firm, to grind into them the kind of conviction that such a statement needed, but the hint of huskiness deflected that effort and she hoped he hadn't noticed it. Boldly, she continued, 'We are just two people who were in need of love and affection and who sought solace in each other's company.'

'Love and affection?' His brows lifted in that sexy way he always looked at her when they were alone, instantly disarming her, and as her pulse leapt she realised her error. This man didn't put any store in love, probably didn't believe in it; lust was all that had mattered to him. The two weeks she'd spent every night in his arms had been just a distraction for him, amusement before he committed to marriage for the benefit of his kingdom. Hadn't their conversation the night she'd arrived in Kezoban proved that?

'Well, affection at least.' Her nerve began to falter, his closeness eroding all her bravado, taking her right back to the beginning, to that first time he'd kissed her after they'd ridden in the desert. 'Love can never be part of it. You have a marriage to make and I have a life to go back to in England.'

He nodded slowly and for a moment she thought she saw something resembling disappointment in his eyes before he looked quickly away into the suite as someone knocked then tried to enter. He gave a command in his language, his voice steady and calm, and she was certain it wasn't an invitation to join them. When he looked back at her, his hard gaze meeting hers, all trace of disappointment had been extinguished; only a fierce intensity remained.

'Were you looking for love, Destiny?' The question threw her off guard almost as much as the sudden seductive tone of his voice. It was like silk over her skin and she stepped back from him, wanting to distance herself emotionally and physically.

'No.' Even to her own ears the denial sounded too fast, too vehement and she quickly backed it up. 'Never that.'

'So affection is all you desire?'

'Yes.' She tried not to think of the fact that she'd given herself so completely to him. She'd given her virginity and her heart exactly because she loved him, even if she hadn't recognised it until now. All she'd known was that being with him had felt right, so very right, and she almost stumbled over the untruth of her next words. 'Just affection.'

'Affection is a very good basis on which to build a marriage.' His voice had softened slightly, knocking her completely off balance. She didn't want to hear about his impending marriage, his affection for his chosen bride, not when she loved him so much.

'Yes, I suppose it is, but nothing has changed, not even with the possibility that I'm pregnant. I have to leave, Zafir. The last thing I want is to jeopardise your marriage.'

Did she want to leave because the thought of him with another woman, taking her as his wife, was too painful? Was it self-protection? Was that why she was so insistent on turning her back on the man she loved?

No. This wasn't about her any more—or Zafir. It

was about the baby they'd created. She had to know for sure if she had inherited her mother's antithrombin deficiency and the only way to do that was to go home to England and have the tests she'd refused, despite being urged by Milly not to. She could still hear herself telling her sister that there was no point, that she didn't want marriage and definitely not children.

'You won't.' He pulled her back to the present and closed the distance she'd created between them and she forced herself to stand still, to remain so close she could smell the desert on him and if she was brave enough to reach out, she would be able to touch him. But the fear she'd lived with, silently hanging over her, now demanded attention.

This was madness. She was in love with a man who didn't even know the concept of the word, a man who took control and power to the ultimate level and, more importantly, a man who was about to marry another woman.

To make matters worse, she was pregnant with his child—one she didn't even know if she could risk having. Her heart ripped in two. Memories of the night she'd been coldly informed she had a new sister but she didn't have a mother clashed painfully with the present.

There was no other option. She had to leave and if it meant putting up a fight then she'd do exactly that.

'There is nothing to discuss, Zafir. We are finished. I'm leaving. Today, tomorrow, I don't care, but I'm leaving.'

'You will not leave.' Zafir held his nerve despite the thud in his chest. He couldn't let her leave. She was carrying his child. The child was the heir he needed but it was more than that, much more. He needed Destiny. He had been hiding from that fact, running like a man scared ever since their first night together.

How could he want a woman so much when he'd denied his sister her chance at love and lost her because of it? Had he gone to Destiny that second night because he'd loved her? Or had it been because he'd wanted to make her his? Either way, he'd buried that emotion so deep beneath his need to do his duty he'd been unable to feel it.

What he felt for her was not just because of the fact that he was the only man to have made love to her. But by giving him her virginity she'd bound them ever tighter, tied them to each other emotionally in a way he'd never known possible and he didn't want to sever those ties. She was his and his alone.

It was that shocking revelation that had brought him back to the palace, forcing him to abandon any thought of an arranged marriage. He wanted only Destiny and as soon as he'd realised what Mina knew he was convinced fate had intervened, salving his conscience slightly. Whatever he'd thought his duty would be, it was clear that now his duty was to the new life they'd created. The heir of Kezoban. The idea of being permanently linked to Destiny, the woman he loved, was one he didn't in the least find unpleasant. Maybe in time she'd learn to love him. Plenty of arranged marriages started with strangers who later become lovers. But they weren't strangers. They had been lovers.

'I *have* to go, Zafir.' The pleading edge in her voice had become tinged with agitation. Was the idea of staying with him that unappealing?

'I will not allow you to leave.' The growl in his

voice made her look cautiously at him, but he had to make her see she couldn't leave. Not now she carried the heir of Kezoban. He intended to make their child legitimate and acknowledge it in every way possible.

'When does your chosen bride arrive?' she asked tartly, pulling his focus back to her face. Her obvious intention of riling him hit its mark. 'I'm sure she wouldn't want to find your mistress lingering here, especially when I'm shrouded in the speculation of pregnancy. I certainly wouldn't want to start a marriage with an illegitimate child in the background.'

'At least that is something we agree on.' He watched as she turned from him to look out over the gardens, dragging her long fingers through her hair in agitation. He wasn't being fair. She was expecting his child and had been unwell for several days. It wouldn't do to distress her further. It was time to make his intentions clear. 'My bride is already here.'

'All the more reason for me to leave right now.' She turned and looked up him and he thought he heard pain in her voice, felt the agony of saying goodbye, but as she began to walk away he knew he'd imagined it and he caught her arm, keeping her close.

His pulse, which still raced after she'd mentioned love and affection, thundered wildly in his head at the thought of what he needed to do. For one foolhardy moment he'd thought she loved him, thought that what they'd shared had been love, but she'd soon backtracked and he knew he couldn't tell her how he felt. Not now.

'You cannot leave, Destiny, not when *you* are my bride.'

She looked at him with wide eyes which never left his face and her teeth bit into her lower lip. The urge to stroke his finger over that spot, to soothe the pain, was so intense he had to let her go and step back or he would be in danger of displaying his true feelings and he hadn't yet begun to understand them.

He should be used to keeping his emotions under wraps, but telling her how he felt, that he couldn't imagine his life without her in it, was hard. He'd never loved anyone before, never experienced love. His mother had returned to her family home when his parents' marriage had broken down, any formal separation impossible, and she'd died a virtual stranger when he was only a teenager. No, he consoled himself, it was far better for Destiny to think he was doing his duty by his child if she herself denounced love so fiercely.

'No,' she said and stumbled back from him, each pace taking her farther away until she was against the wide archway over the large doors to the garden. 'I can't marry you.'

'You can and you will. Tomorrow's feast of thanks to you will now become our engagement. By nightfall the kingdom will know and before the moon rises full and bright over the desert, you will be my wife.'

'Are you mad?' she gasped out, her head shaking in denial. 'We can't possibly marry.'

'You are carrying my child, my heir, and I have never been saner in my life.'

CHAPTER ELEVEN

'No. I CAN'T.' Destiny tried hard to stop her limbs trembling as she faced the man she'd fallen in love with, the man who was the father of the new life inside her—the man she *had* to leave. She had no option. The only thing she could do was return home and have the tests and for that she'd need Milly's support.

He moved towards her, fierce and powerful, every stride bringing her into contact with that powerful aura. 'The child you carry is my heir, Destiny, and you will not keep me from my duty as a father. Neither will you leave Kezoban.'

'You can't keep me here, not when I want nothing other than to go back to my life and leave you to do what you should do. You must make the marriage you'd planned on.' She knew her voice was trembling and that each word was barely a whisper.

'The child is my heir, Destiny.' His deep voice was more of a low guttural growl and she bit down hard on her lower lip again, trying to find even the smallest hint of inner strength. Nothing. Every drop of determination had left her, swept away as quickly as if a sandstorm had raged through the room.

'You need to marry for the good of your country and

I'm not that, Zafir. I never have been and never will be.'
She had to make him see how impossible his sugges-
tion was. It tugged on her heartstrings to think that he
wanted her as his wife but she couldn't marry a Sheikh,
the ruler of a kingdom. She was not of his world and
didn't belong here but, worse than that, she wouldn't
marry him just because he felt duty-bound to do so.

Zafir glared at her. 'There is a greater honour at
stake now, a far more important duty to be done. One
that is much greater than my country. That duty is first
and foremost to my child.'

He moved closer and she pressed herself back
against the door, as if the heat of the fire had leapt out
at her. 'No.' She couldn't say any more, couldn't tell
him she didn't want him to feel any sense of obligation towards her or the baby. She didn't want him to be
forced to alter his life and certainly didn't want him to
be forced to marry her out of duty because of their baby.

Their baby.

She gulped back the raw emotion that rushed at her
from the past. She didn't know if she could do this, any
of it. Just by becoming pregnant and making a man
duty-bound to ask her to marry him she was repeating
so much of her mother's history. What if she repeated
the rest? What if she encountered the same problems
during the birth and left the baby alone in the world?
Would he be so keen to do his duty then? Her father
hadn't. He might have provided for her and Milly, but
every bit had been grudging and he'd ruled with an iron
rod of annoyance at being a single father. She couldn't
risk her child growing up like that.

These thoughts made her head spin, but she couldn't
give in. She had to convince Zafir he didn't have any

obligations towards her. The only reason she would ever have for marrying him was love—and that was something he scorned.

'Why did you keep your condition a secret?'

'Condition?' *How did he know?* 'What condition?'

'The baby. Why didn't you tell me?'

'I didn't want to say anything until I'd seen a doctor—until I knew it was certain.' His suspicion filled the air, the room heavy with it.

'You do not need to go back to England to do that. I will arrange all the medical care you need. As my wife you will have nothing but the best.'

Destiny's temper rose as she realised she'd jumped to conclusions. He didn't know she might be advised against having the baby but it did make everything he said even clearer. He was asking her to marry him out of a sense of duty. She retaliated, tapping into the strength she'd discovered when she'd struck her deal with him at home in England—anything was better than being forced into a marriage neither of them wanted, especially when she needed to go back home and try to find peace of mind.

'I didn't tell you because the deal we struck was for two weeks, not the rest of my life.'

Fury filled those dark eyes, making them narrow in anger. 'The deal we struck?' The incredulity in his voice was clear and it cut through her dying heart, but it was for the best. If he thought she was so mercenary that she'd use her pregnancy to barter with him, then he would send her from Kezoban faster than she could gather her packed bags.

As he looked at her, his eyes glittering and hard, fear prickled over her. What would he do next? Would he shout at her, march from the room after a torrent of heated abuse, just as she'd often seen her father do with her stepmother? Yet more proof that love needed to be the only reason for a marriage.

Instead he pulled out the chair from the table set in the shade of the terrace of her suite. With deliberate slowness he sat, leant back, placed his elbows on the arms of the chair and linked his tanned fingers together in front of his chest. The cold discipline was so unexpected she could only stare at him, unable to say anything.

'Sit.' The command was strong, his voice firm, the icy deliberateness of it a total contrast to the cooling heat of the sun as it began to sink lower over the desert beyond the palace walls, but still she ignored it, standing defiantly.

'We have much to discuss and I will not begin until you sit.' The aura of power shrouded him like a cloak and, even though she had nothing to discuss, she pulled out the other chair and sat opposite him, crossing her arms over her stomach, as if to protect the life within. He glanced down at her arms, a flicker of annoyance on his handsome face, then he looked back up at her, his eyes colder than she'd ever seen them.

'Nothing you can say will change my mind, Zafir.'

'If our time together has been about your financial gain, I will make a deal with you now that will ensure you live in luxury for the rest of your life, provided our child is raised as the legitimate heir to the kingdom of Kezoban.'

The coldness of his voice told her she'd been successful in touching that open nerve she'd uncovered. He was so furious, ice-cold, almost devoid of any trace of emotion. But she had one more blow to deliver, one that hurt her to think of it, let alone say it, but it was born of the fear from that last entry in her mother's diary.

'Even that generous offer will not change my mind, not when I do not want this baby.' By saying those words aloud it quelled all her fears, making her want to do anything to protect the tiny life inside her, even if it meant she had to ignore the love she had for this man.

As that callous admission left her lips she knew that, whatever she had to face, she would have this baby. Milly would be with her all the way and if the test results proved to be positive and she faced the worst, she would insist her sister brought up the baby. That way it would at least be loved, because Milly longed for marriage and children. That was why she'd bravely taken the test when she herself had shied away from it.

'I see.' His calm acceptance of the admission of her darkest fear was almost too much. 'So a deal which means you can leave Kezoban after the child is born would be mutually beneficial.'

'What?' She jumped up, sending her chair scraping across the marble floor of the terrace.

'I will pay you whatever amount you name to remain in Kezoban as my wife until the child is born.'

'I'm not leaving my baby here. What kind of woman do you think I am?' Did he really think she was that heartless? But wasn't that exactly what she'd wanted him to think? Now she wished she'd never said anything. She should have kept her fears to herself and just left.

'I believe you are the kind of woman who will want only the best for your child, and the best will be for him to be brought up here, in the palace, as a future ruler of his country.' Zafir still sat watching her, his hands remaining calmly linked before him, but the scrutiny in his eyes left her in no doubt that he was aware of every flicker of emotion she was trying to hide.

The ground beneath her feet seemed to move and her body swayed as if she had been aboard a ship for many days. She sat down quickly, not wanting him to guess her weakness. The only option she had right now was to agree to his outlandish terms in order to end this discussion. Tomorrow she would have to convince him that the only way forward was to allow her to return to England.

She swallowed hard. 'If the deal is right, then I will agree.'

'The deal will be right, make no mistake about that, and tomorrow at the feast our engagement will be announced.'

The next day Zafir was still mad with rage at how mercenary and calculated Destiny had been, bargaining with their child as if it was nothing more than an inconvenience she needed to be rid of. Just a few days ago, he'd thought he'd fallen in love with her, an emotion he had never experienced before, but how could he love someone so cold? All she'd done was string him along, lead him to believe there was something between them, when really she'd been working towards her ultimate goal of striking a deal that would set her up for life.

Whatever she did or said, there was no escaping the fact that now there was something between them, something he suspected she hadn't planned for. A child. His child—and he would do a deal with the devil himself if it meant he could keep his son or daughter in Kezoban and in his life. In just a few hours he would make the announcement that would seal that deal and tell his people that Destiny was to be his bride. He knew it would cause problems. She was different—but she was the mother of his heir, a fact which changed everything.

She was also the woman he'd fallen in love with and he'd come back to tell her that he wanted only her, but the realisation that she was carrying his child changed things. Emotions were no longer important. Love or hate didn't play any part in the deal he'd just struck with her. Duty was the driving force.

Zafir sat in his lavish banquet room, looking out over his people, but he was more distracted than he'd ever been. His attention kept flitting to the grand arched doors, waiting for Destiny's arrival. Still raw from her painful admission that she didn't want his child, he couldn't believe that he longed to see her, that more than anything he wanted to hold her and kiss her again.

He had to constantly remind himself that she was not who he'd thought she was. Her harsh admissions yesterday burned in his soul, dimming the love he had for her, but obviously it had not subdued the lust and desire. If she'd hoped to escape him she'd played it all wrong. Those admissions made him more determined to keep her in Kezoban and make her his wife.

Finally, as the great banquet room thronged with the elite of his kingdom, he saw her. The thump in his chest, as if he'd been hit by a weapon, caught him off guard. She looked pale, her dark eyes almost too big as she glanced around the room. Had she slept or had she tossed all night as he had?

Around the room the hum of conversation dipped to a curious whisper and he knew that was down to the lavish deep purple and gold silks she wore, exactly as he'd instructed Mina to ensure. They were his colours and marked her as his.

Across the room her gaze met his and, over the heads of his people, that spark which always sizzled when he saw her leapt to life once more. Nothing, it seemed, could dim that. He stood up on the raised platform and gestured her to be escorted to him. The guests parted as she made her way towards him, the whispers becoming more intense as a sense of expectancy filled the room.

She joined him on the platform and he took her hand, which alone spoke volumes to his people. He stood beside her and began to address everyone in Arabic, aware of her nervousness. Beside him she trembled but he continued to speak, putting out his arm to her in presentation as his announcement stunned those gathered before them into silence. For her benefit he repeated his words in English.

'Meet the woman I intend to marry, a woman from far away but whose very name, Destiny, suggests fate has sent her here to be at my side as my wife.'

As speculative whispers raced around the room he looked at Destiny. Her dark eyes, so soft and gentle, regarded him warily and he wished he could do more to allay her fears. He wanted to hold her close, kiss her beautiful face, but protocol needed to be followed. Their union had to be above question or reproach if his people were ever to accept it.

A cheer went up from the back of the room, followed by more, and relief flooded him. 'You are being received well.' He spoke in hushed tones, leaning close to her. 'My people like and approve of you.'

'When they discover the truth, they may not be so pleased with your decision to break with tradition and marry an outsider.' She spoke as softly as he had, keeping a smile on her face, an outward sign of happiness. Already she was performing the role of Kezoban royalty well.

'My people are happy. They see that you have made me happy, taken away the dark cloud which hung over us after Tabinah's accident. To them it is a love match.' He inhaled as he said those last words, catching the scent of her, filling his mind and his body with a rush of need, laced with guilt. He had no right to be happy, no right to feel the way he did for this woman, but it was an illusion he now had to live under—for the sake of his child.

'And what happens when they discover the truth about the baby?' Anger rushed forward, pushing aside guilt or need at her hard but whispered words. He had no idea what his people would say or do, when she followed through with their deal and left Kezoban, left him and their child after the birth. That was the only flaw in his plan, but he wouldn't worry over that now.

'All they need to know at present is that we shall be married within the week.'

'Within the week?' Destiny could hardly speak. When she'd made that deal with Zafir the day before, it had all been about ending the circles they were talking in, giving her time to be alone and think of what she re-

ally needed to do. But marriage within a week—that
had not been part of the deal. She couldn't marry him,
even if she knew the test would be clear; she couldn't
link herself to this man for evermore. But hadn't that
link already been created?

'We cannot talk here. I will come to you later.' A
rush of activity heralded the beginning of the feast as
music struck up and people settled down to eat, entertained by dancers. It was so far removed from anything
she'd ever seen it was almost possible to think it was
a dream, but it was very real. Somehow, she'd struck
a deal with this man, one she secretly loved, to be his
wife, but she'd never anticipated it would be so soon.
She was trapped.

Mina approached them with a young woman at her
side who offered her a single white flower. It was tall
and elegant, its petals silky-soft as Destiny took it and
smiled her thanks.

She almost jumped when Zafir's deep seductive
voice whispered close to her ear, 'It is a symbol of
fertility.'

She looked at him, wishing he wasn't so close, so
dangerously attractive. 'She knows.'

Zafir smiled at her, the first genuine smile that made
his eyes sparkle in a way she hadn't seen since the
morning he'd left her bed for the last time. 'You have
a friend and loyal servant in Mina.'

Destiny turned again to Mina, bowing her head
slightly, and offered her thanks, wishing she'd had time
to learn a few basic Arabic phrases, as 'thank you' in
English didn't quite convey her full gratitude.

For the next two hours, Zafir stayed diligently at
her side as more token gifts were bestowed on her. The

feasting grew noisier as people enjoyed the excuse to celebrate but Destiny couldn't relax, not with Zafir's threat of seeking her out later in her mind. What did he want now? They had already agreed on how to proceed, or rather he had told her how it would be. He had taken control. How could she expect anything less from a man such as Zafir?

'Mina will escort you to your suite.' Zafir's words caught her attention as she watched the dancers, their exotic moves making her wish she could be as carefree as them. Maybe if she was, then she might have snared Zafir's heart. As she looked up at him, his next words sent her emotions and her pulse rate completely off balance. 'I will join you as soon as I can.'

Destiny knew this would be the final chance she had of settling things between them and, whatever he did, she would break off the engagement and leave. 'Should Mina stay, for propriety?'

She couldn't keep the challenge from her voice, couldn't help goading him, and the narrowing of his eyes told her she'd achieved her aim. She must not give him the chance to talk softly to her, in that sexy tone which made her forget all her worries. She couldn't let it happen. The only way she could see of leaving without any further implications was to antagonise him, push him so far he'd forget all about those hot nights when desire had claimed them both.

'Mina will guard your secret well, just as she has been doing since our first night together. She believes we are in love and will do anything to help bring us together in marriage.' The silky-soft tone of his voice was as challenging as her sharp words of moments ago.

'Then I see I have little choice.' Before he had a

chance to form a reply she turned and walked from him, following Mina, who had been waiting to escort her back to her suite. Why did everything he said and did become a hurdle to climb over? No wonder Tabinah had run away. His need to control was overpowering.

CHAPTER TWELVE

ZAFIR STOOD OUTSIDE Destiny's suite, bracing himself for the battle he knew he was about to face. Something was troubling her and he intended to find out exactly what it was, then remove that issue so that they could unite in marriage, enabling his child to be born in Kezoban and grow up as a future ruler within the bounds of a happy marriage. Maybe he did have to put his heart on the line, tell her how he felt. If he did, could she love him? The passion they'd shared made it plausible, but was it possible to force someone to love you?

He didn't knock but strode in to find her standing in the middle of the suite, arms folded tightly, still wearing the deep purple and gold silks he'd sent for her. He didn't even have the chance to close the door as her first words hurtled at him like a missile.

'I don't want to marry you.' Her defiance, if it wasn't so infuriating, would have been remarkable. She looked stunning, standing beneath the bright lights of the suite, her eyes flaming with anger and mistrust. But why? How had what they'd shared turned so sour?

'The marriage is arranged. The announcement has been made. It cannot be undone. Next week you will be my wife.' He clenched his hands in fury at the humiliation of being told he wasn't good enough for her, that *she* didn't want *him*. 'It is my duty to my child to marry you.'

'Duty?' She gasped the question out at him and for a second he reeled with shock. Nobody had ever addressed him so, but he should be more accustomed to it from this woman by now.

He strode over to her, intent on making her see that marriage was the only option, that he would not have his child born out of wedlock and, worse still, in a foreign land. His duty was to his kingdom and producing an heir was part of that duty. Now that he knew she carried his child, he would do all it took to protect that heir.

'Yes, duty. Something you are not at all familiar with.' He recalled the challenging look she'd given her stepmother the first time they'd met.

'How dare you?' she hurled at him in indignation.

'I dare because I will do anything for my child.' He matched her anger with cool reserve, knowing now more than ever he needed to remain in control. It wasn't right to upset her, not when she carried his child.

'A child I can't give you.' The quiver of desperation in her voice wasn't quite masked by her fury; if anything, it only revealed that there was much more to what she'd said than just those words.

'You are talking riddles. Speak plainly.' He narrowed his eyes, not sure what was coming next, but preparing to counteract it swiftly.

'Very well.' Her tone was flippant, her stance defiant and he resisted the urge to hold her arms and force her to look into his eyes in the hope that he could remind her of the passion and desire which had brought them together. He wanted to see that again, to know they could be like that once more. 'I cannot have your baby, Zafir, simply because I don't want to.'

A furious red rage fogged his mind. He'd thought they'd settled this. 'What are you saying?'

'That I cannot have the baby.'

An icy shard stabbed at his heart. Whatever the reason for such a bald and cold statement, he had to know it, had to find a way to fight it. 'I will not allow you to do anything to my child and, if necessary, I will not let you out of my sight until it is safely born.'

'It could cost me my life.' The pain-racked sob which broke from her froze him to the spot. The raw agony in her eyes made him hurt, as if an unknown force was squeezing his chest so tight he couldn't breathe. Memories of the night he'd lost Tabinah, of the guilt he'd carried ever since, mixed with the thought of losing Destiny. For the second time in as many days he faced the thought of life without her. He knew that life without the woman he loved would be impossible.

He couldn't lose her, not now he'd found her.

He lowered his voice to a gentle whisper, letting go of all the anger she'd provoked in him, sensing a genuine need, a real cry for help from within her. 'How do you know this?'

'My mother...' she swallowed down hard and when she continued her voice was a cracked whisper loaded with pain and fear '...she died soon after giving birth to my little sister—because of a hereditary disease.'

Why hadn't she confessed her fears from the outset? Now her unwillingness to tell him she'd become pregnant was finally beginning to make sense. Gently he took her hand and led her to the cushions of the seating area, urging her to sit. Then he too sat and, holding her hands in his, cautiously continued, 'What happened, Destiny?'

'It's a condition called antithrombin deficiency. She didn't even know she had it and each pregnancy increases the risk to the mother.' She looked up at him, tears shining in her eyes, and he fought hard against the need to hold her, to soothe her pain. This was something she needed to talk about first. His mind whirled. He had already alerted his physician to her pregnancy and he would know exactly what to do. He would give her nothing but the best medical care.

'She kept a diary but never made another entry after Milly was born.'

'And that is why you don't want our baby? You think you will be the same?' He fought against the need to hold her tight, to infuse her with all the love he had for her in his heart in an attempt to heal her pain. But she'd told him she'd never wanted love and if he confessed his true feelings it might be too much—for her and the baby. 'Can tests be performed to determine your health?'

'Yes.' She looked down at her hands, unable to maintain the contact they'd had over the last few minutes, and his heart felt crushed. She didn't trust him enough to share it with him. How could he ever make their marriage happy if she didn't trust him?

'Why have you not been tested?'

She looked back up at him and the pain in her eyes wrenched at him, tearing him to pieces. He just wanted to make it right for her. But could he?

'Milly had the test because she's always wanted to

get married and have children, but I've never been tested.'

His eyes narrowed. 'Because you didn't want children?'

'Or marriage.' The cracked whisper of her voice was more shocking than her admission. He was forcing her to do the very things she was trying to avoid and the fact that she was carrying his child was due to his mistake. He vividly remembered that first night when she'd had to remind him to use protection. All her pain now was his fault. He'd done this to her.

'I've done everything as my mother did. She fell in love with a man who didn't love her and then she was forced into marriage because of pregnancy.'

Her words dragged him back, but they were like a spear through his heart. She'd fallen in love with another man, one who didn't want her. Was that why she'd spent that first night with him, giving him something he didn't deserve? She'd been using him, using the powerful attraction between them to wipe away the memories of another man?

He couldn't focus on that revelation now; he had to keep in mind that the child she carried, the one she didn't want for fear of becoming ill like her mother, was his child, his heir.

'I will give you the best medical care in the world. You can have all the tests you need to ensure you and the baby will be healthy, but you will stay and become my wife. We can raise our child together, or you can leave after it's born, but it must be born within the bounds of wedlock if it is to be recognised as a true heir to the throne of Kezobàn.'

'What if I can't keep the baby? What if the test is positive?' The fear in her voice was clear.

'Once you have the test we will know the situation.' His mind whirled with the implications of what she'd told him. He could lose his child but, far worse, he could lose the woman he loved and if he couldn't admit to her what he felt, he couldn't turn his back on her. He wanted to be with her as she found out. He wanted to help her through whatever came after—no matter what the results were. He wanted her because he loved her. Every second he looked into her eyes intensified that.

'I'm scared.' The hushed whisper held hints of shame and he fought against the urge to hold her, protect her from fear, but just by doing that he could scare her more.

'There is nothing to be scared of, Destiny. Not now. I'll be with you all the way. We'll deal with this together.'

'Why?' Confusion clouded her eyes and filled her voice.

'You are to be my wife, Destiny.'

'But I still couldn't marry you, don't you see?'

He shook his head, unable to comprehend what more she wanted.

'I know what it's like to grow up at the mercy of a man who never wanted to be a husband, much less a father.' She lowered her gaze and pulled her hand free of his, clutching hers tightly in her lap. 'I cannot do that to you, Zafir. I am not your destiny.'

All was becoming clear to him. While he'd been nursing his guilt about what had happened to Tabinah, she'd been running scared. Just as he'd lost Tabinah, he could have lost Destiny. The way he'd felt when he'd realised she'd taken Majeed into the desert rushed back at him, taking all the breath and strength from his body.

'I can't let you go, Destiny.' The truth of his emotions ripped from him, his words lacking any of his usual firm control, and she looked at him questioningly. Had he finally got through to her, finally made her see why he couldn't let her go?

'It doesn't change anything.' Sadness echoed in every word.

She took a small faltering step towards him but her next words destroyed any hope. He couldn't give up on her because he loved her.

'Even if you looked into the future and predicted I'd be in the best of health and give birth to a healthy baby, I still couldn't marry you.'

'Don't you see, Destiny, you gifted me your virginity and, even if that union hadn't resulted in a child, I am duty-bound by my honour to marry you? It is the way of my country.'

'But I was never a candidate to be your wife, I was just a passing affair, your last mistress before you married. You even went in search of a wife. Your honour didn't stop that. So what's changed?'

Zafir recalled how he'd felt as he'd met with the women who were presented to him. In each and every face he'd looked for Destiny. He'd longed for her as he'd lain alone in bed; she was all he could think about and because of that he'd halted his search. Even before he'd known she carried his child, he was sure she was the one, the woman he wanted to be his bride.

The very fact that he had chosen her and not let his

aides decide was an issue he couldn't get past initially. Was he right to seek marriage to the woman of his choice when he had forced Tabinah into an arranged marriage—making her so unhappy she had run away, losing her life in the process?

Now, to add to the confusion filling his mind and his heart, Destiny had admitted that she'd slept with him because she'd been spurned by the man she loved. Was the pain in his heart, the ache in his soul because he too had been rejected by the person he loved? Destiny couldn't love him because she loved another man.

He stood up, knowing he couldn't force her to love him, couldn't force her to stay. Her heart belonged to another man. He couldn't force his will on another woman. He'd done that to his sister and had learnt from it. He loved Destiny too much and he would do anything for her—even let her go.

'I have made you unhappy, just as I did to Tabinah. I will give anything you need, but please know that you are free to go, free to make your own choices. I will not force you to do anything.' The pain those words caused burned like fire in his throat, making them almost impossible to say.

'What of your duty to your country, your people?' Her face had paled and he worried he would upset her, make her ill.

'My duty is still to my country and my people, but it is also to the child we created out of love and affection.' He was testing, gauging her reaction to the mention of the emotions she'd already denied wanting from him. Now he knew why—because her heart belonged to another—but his heart belonged to her and if she left she'd take it with her.

* * *

Destiny's body, weary from the constant battle of wills, went rigid with anger. How could he say they'd shared love and affection? He'd already made it perfectly clear he didn't want anything to do with such feelings. He was just saying it now as a last-ditch attempt at keeping her in Kezoban.

'It wasn't love, Zafir, it was lust. Pure carnal lust.'

'Can you be so sure?' He came to stand before her, forcing her to look up at him and intensifying his domination, a tactic used often by her father. She stood quickly in an attempt to counteract it. 'Maybe it was lust that brought us together, but what if it is now something more? Can you turn your back on that?'

'Saying it isn't enough.' She hated that he was taunting her again.

'Then I will show you.'

Before she could do anything she was in his arms, her body responding as his lips met hers in a hard and demanding kiss. Fire leapt to life within her, scorching her heart and, try as she might, she couldn't stop her arms winding around his neck, keeping her close to his lean body. The need which rushed through her was so wild, so intense she could hardly breathe.

His hands cradled her head, keeping her in exactly the right place, enabling him to delve deeper with his kiss, pushing her further towards the edge. Sense suddenly prevailed and she pulled her arms from his neck, pushing hard against him.

Finally he let her go and she staggered backwards, her body pulsing with desire that would have to remain unquenched for evermore.

'That proves nothing but lust. It proves that I am

nothing more than a convenient mistress. I want more, Zafir, more than that.' She hated her ragged breathing as she fought for control and the heated flush of her cheeks.

Zafir too was breathing hard but his face wore an expression she'd never seen before. He looked vulnerable and exposed, as if he'd finally smashed down every barrier around him.

'What do you want?' The husky growl of his voice sent a tingle of awareness down her spine.

'I want a marriage made out of love.'

'Love will flourish if you let it—if you forget the man you claim to have given your love to and open your heart to one who does love you.'

Now she was confused. Was the passion he'd set free within her fogging her mind, mixing with the worry of the test she knew she had to face, making her imagine things? 'What man?'

'You said you'd done the same as your mother— fallen in love with a man who didn't love you.'

He took hold of her arms, pulling her closer to him, the fire of unsated desire sparking around them. *Open your heart to one who does love you.* Those words echoed in her mind but she was too scared to say anything. What if she'd got it wrong? It was bad enough he thought she loved someone else, but if she exposed her love for him, would he use it as a weapon to make her stay?

'Who is this man?' A hint of jealousy showed in his voice and she knew she had to be totally honest with him, risking her heart in the process if she'd got it wrong.

'He is a great leader, a very powerful man, exactly the kind of man I did not want to love.'

'Who is he, Destiny?'

'You.'

The silence which followed that one word was so tangible it was as if a mist had shrouded them, but the expression on his face rushed from disbelief to suspicion. He didn't believe her.

'Why?'

'Why what?' Did he mean why did she love him? Or why was he the wrong man for her?

'Why do you not want to love a man such as myself, to quote your words, a great leader, a very powerful man?'

'Because I have spent twenty-six years being ruled by a man who didn't have even the smallest amount of love inside him for me, his daughter. I have protected my sister, who is prone to speaking her mind, more times than I can remember from his wrath. He is only happy when he is controlling those around him. I came here because I cannot live any longer like that. The deal I made with you was my escape route.'

Zafir looked at Destiny, shocked not just by the admission that she loved him, but by the story of her childhood. No wonder she'd made that overzealous deal with him. She'd been desperate to get away from the man who was supposed to protect her. Her father.

'It is true I am a leader, but a leader of my people for the good of my country. I would never seek to dominate one person—not again.'

'Again?'

'Why do you think Tabinah left? Why did she ride

out on my horse, a beast that was far too strong for her to handle? Because I forced her into marriage, forced her away from a man she'd grown up with, one I've since discovered she wanted to marry. It was to him she was riding and planning to run away with. My need to control her made that happen.'

All the guilt poured out in those words. He should never have insisted Tabinah make that marriage. This was the twenty-first century and time for change. He should have seen that her heart was already taken. He'd lost her and he'd thought the same of Destiny when she'd said she'd given her heart to a man who couldn't love her and what he'd said afterwards had come from deep within his heart. He did love her.

Destiny's silence said it all. She was probably wishing she'd never admitted loving him.

'I see my words have proved you right. I am the all-controlling man you fear.' He let her arms go and turned from her, not wanting to see the accusation in her eyes. He had to leave, to walk away. He'd played it all wrong. Gambled and lost.

'Zafir.'

The softness of her voice stilled the thud of his heart and he turned to look at her, but remained silent.

'It wasn't your fault. Tabinah's accident.'

'How can you be so sure?'

'When love is involved, all sense or reason disappears. Whatever you'd have done, it wouldn't have been enough. Love can make you do crazy things, such as agreeing to marry a desert Sheikh and staying with him.'

He frowned and strode back to her. As she looked up into his face he saw love blazing from her eyes, so bright and vibrant he knew he'd found the one person who would always have his heart. His Destiny.

'You really mean that?'

'Yes, but what about the test? What happens if I have inherited the same condition which claimed my mother's life?'

'Together we can face anything, Destiny. I love you. Nothing else matters. I want you in my life as my wife for ever.'

'What if I can't have children? What of your duty to your country then?'

'Don't worry about that now. My physician will give you the very best care.'

'Then I can face anything if I have your love, because I love you, Zafir, so very much.'

He swept her from her feet, gathering her up in his arms, and made his way out of her suite, along the corridor of his palace, totally heedless of any servants.

'Where are we going?' The question held a hint of teasing and he looked down at her, his eyes devouring the softness of her face.

'To the Sheikh's suite.'

'What will people think? What about protocol?'

'They will think I'm madly in love with you—and they will be right.'

EPILOGUE

'I HAVE A gift for you.' Zafir's voice sent a shimmer of desire down Destiny's spine as he stood behind her, pulling her against his body.

She looked out over the palace gardens and to the desert beyond. So much had happened in the year she'd been here. Her life was so complete—married to the man she loved with a baby son who was the centre of their world. The fear of the tests was just a blurry memory now she knew she hadn't inherited anything from her mother other than the need to be loved.

In just a few hours, her sister would be arriving for what was fast becoming a regular monthly visit. How could she possibly need or want more?

'I don't need gifts, Zafir.' She turned in his arms to look up at him. 'I have more than I can ever want.'

He kissed her gently, his lips holding the promise of much more pleasure. 'This one I think you will want.'

He took her by the hand and led her from the suite, towards the stables.

'Why are we going this way? Have you bought another horse?'

His smile was full of love and it melted her heart all over again. 'You know me too well.'

Intent on pleasing Zafir, she walked with him, but when they entered the ornate stables she was astonished to see Milly.

'What are you doing here? I thought you weren't due to arrive until this evening.'

'Change of plan.' Her sister grinned as she opened a stable door. Destiny looked in and gasped. The bay mare contentedly eating hay was Ellie, the young horse her father had forced her to sell. She stroked the familiar silky coat and the mare responded, nuzzling against her in recognition.

'How did you find her?' She turned to Zafir, a strange urge to cry almost overwhelming her.

'With Milly's help.'

Destiny looked at her sister. 'How did you manage to keep it a secret?'

'With great difficulty.'

Zafir took her hands, pulling her to him, and she looked up into his eyes. 'Exactly a year ago, you arrived in Kezoban. You brought sunshine and the hope of a new beginning to my life and I wanted to celebrate that. What better gift than the horse you were forced to part with?'

Destiny smiled up at Zafir. 'I love you, Sheikh Zafir Al Asmari, so very much.'

'And I love you, my very own Destiny.'

* * * * *

MILLS & BOON®
Hardback – May 2016

ROMANCE

Morelli's Mistress	Anne Mather
A Tycoon to Be Reckoned With	Julia James
Billionaire Without a Past	Carol Marinelli
The Shock Cassano Baby	Andie Brock
The Most Scandalous Ravensdale	Melanie Milburne
The Sheikh's Last Mistress	Rachael Thomas
Claiming the Royal Innocent	Jennifer Hayward
Kept at the Argentine's Command	Lucy Ellis
The Billionaire Who Saw Her Beauty	Rebecca Winters
In the Boss's Castle	Jessica Gilmore
One Week with the French Tycoon	Christy McKellen
Rafael's Contract Bride	Nina Milne
Tempted by Hollywood's Top Doc	Louisa George
Perfect Rivals...	Amy Ruttan
English Rose in the Outback	Lucy Clark
A Family for Chloe	Lucy Clark
The Doctor's Baby Secret	Scarlet Wilson
Married for the Boss's Baby	Susan Carlisle
Twins for the Texan	Charlene Sands
Secret Baby Scandal	Joanne Rock

GEN STD HB

MILLS & BOON®
Large Print – May 2016

ROMANCE

The Queen's New Year Secret	Maisey Yates
Wearing the De Angelis Ring	Cathy Williams
The Cost of the Forbidden	Carol Marinelli
Mistress of His Revenge	Chantelle Shaw
Theseus Discovers His Heir	Michelle Smart
The Marriage He Must Keep	Dani Collins
Awakening the Ravensdale Heiress	Melanie Milburne
His Princess of Convenience	Rebecca Winters
Holiday with the Millionaire	Scarlet Wilson
The Husband She'd Never Met	Barbara Hannay
Unlocking Her Boss's Heart	Christy McKellen

HISTORICAL

In Debt to the Earl	Elizabeth Rolls
Rake Most Likely to Seduce	Bronwyn Scott
The Captain and His Innocent	Lucy Ashford
Scoundrel of Dunborough	Margaret Moore
One Night with the Viking	Harper St. George

MEDICAL

A Touch of Christmas Magic	Scarlet Wilson
Her Christmas Baby Bump	Robin Gianna
Winter Wedding in Vegas	Janice Lynn
One Night Before Christmas	Susan Carlisle
A December to Remember	Sue MacKay
A Father This Christmas?	Louisa Heaton

MILLS & BOON®
Hardback – June 2016

ROMANCE

Bought for the Greek's Revenge	Lynne Graham
An Heir to Make a Marriage	Abby Green
The Greek's Nine-Month Redemption	Maisey Yates
Expecting a Royal Scandal	Caitlin Crews
Return of the Untamed Billionaire	Carol Marinelli
Signed Over to Santino	Maya Blake
Wedded, Bedded, Betrayed	Michelle Smart
The Surprise Conti Child	Tara Pammi
The Greek's Nine-Month Surprise	Jennifer Faye
A Baby to Save Their Marriage	Scarlet Wilson
Stranded with Her Rescuer	Nikki Logan
Expecting the Fellani Heir	Lucy Gordon
The Prince and the Midwife	Robin Gianna
His Pregnant Sleeping Beauty	Lynne Marshall
One Night, Twin Consequences	Annie O'Neil
Twin Surprise for the Single Doc	Susanne Hampton
The Doctor's Forbidden Fling	Karin Baine
The Army Doc's Secret Wife	Charlotte Hawkes
A Pregnancy Scandal	Kat Cantrell
A Bride for the Boss	Maureen Child

MILLS & BOON®
Large Print – June 2016

ROMANCE

Leonetti's Housekeeper Bride	Lynne Graham
The Surprise De Angelis Baby	Cathy Williams
Castelli's Virgin Widow	Caitlin Crews
The Consequence He Must Claim	Dani Collins
Helios Crowns His Mistress	Michelle Smart
Illicit Night with the Greek	Susanna Carr
The Sheikh's Pregnant Prisoner	Tara Pammi
Saved by the CEO	Barbara Wallace
Pregnant with a Royal Baby!	Susan Meier
A Deal to Mend Their Marriage	Michelle Douglas
Swept into the Rich Man's World	Katrina Cudmore

HISTORICAL

Marriage Made in Rebellion	Sophia James
A Too Convenient Marriage	Georgie Lee
Redemption of the Rake	Elizabeth Beacon
Saving Marina	Lauri Robinson
The Notorious Countess	Liz Tyner

MEDICAL

Playboy Doc's Mistletoe Kiss	Tina Beckett
Her Doctor's Christmas Proposal	Louisa George
From Christmas to Forever?	Marion Lennox
A Mummy to Make Christmas	Susanne Hampton
Miracle Under the Mistletoe	Jennifer Taylor
His Christmas Bride-to-Be	Abigail Gordon

MILLS & BOON®

Why shop at millsandboon.co.uk?

Each year, thousands of romance readers find their perfect read at millsandboon.co.uk. That's because we're passionate about bringing you the very best romantic fiction. Here are some of the advantages of shopping at www.millsandboon.co.uk:

* **Get new books first**—you'll be able to buy your favourite books one month before they hit the shops

* **Get exclusive discounts**—you'll also be able to buy our specially created monthly collections, with up to 50% off the RRP

* **Find your favourite authors**—latest news, interviews and new releases for all your favourite authors and series on our website, plus ideas for what to try next

* **Join in**—once you've bought your favourite books, don't forget to register with us to rate, review and join in the discussions

Visit **www.millsandboon.co.uk**
for all this and more today!